NUCLEAR WAR

The Final Battle

Elliot Thornbridge

Copyright © 2025 Daniel Schröder; Elliot Thornbridge

All rights reserved

The characters and events portrayed in this book are fictitious. Any similarity to real persons, living or dead, is coincidental and not intended by the author.

No part of this book may be reproduced, or stored in a retrieval system, or transmitted in any form or by any means, electronic, mechanical, photocopying, recording, or otherwise, without express written permission of the publisher.

Cover design by: Daniel Schröder

Copyright © 2025 Daniel Schröder; Elliot Thornbridge
Dr. Konrad Adeanauerring 13
79787 Lauchringen

CONTENTS

Title Page
Copyright
Chapter 1: Whispers of War   1
Chapter 2: The World on the Brink   20
Chapter 3: The Escape   26
Chapter 4: Destination Paris   39
Chapter 5: The Ultimatum   45
Chapter 6: The Exchange Begins   56
Chapter 7: The Traffic Jam   66
Chapter 8: The Cities Disappear   75
Chapter 9: The Beginning of the End of the World   86
Chapter 10: Arrival   100
Chapter 11: Flight AF4011   132
Chapter 12: The Darkness Underground   142
Chapter 13: Awakening   158
Chapter 14: Are they still alive?   170

Epilogue: A World of Ashes 190

CHAPTER 1: WHISPERS OF WAR

London, November 17, 2025

A thin ray of sunlight crept through the cream-colored curtains of the small suburban house in Croydon, south of London. Eva Thompson glanced briefly at the window as she expertly cracked another egg on the edge of the dark gray cast-iron pan. It was 8:30 on a Tuesday morning that began like any other—with the familiar sizzle of egg yolk hitting the hot surface of the pan.

The forty-one-year-old Eva had tied her long, raven-black hair into a practical ponytail with a simple white hair tie. A few rebellious strands had escaped and framed her slender face with its high cheekbones. She was an attractive woman—slim and athletic, with a small button nose and alert, dark brown eyes that often sparkled with humor. Today, however, her gaze seemed distant, almost worried.

Her husband David had already left two hours ago. Like every morning, he had dragged himself out of bed at 6:30, hastily showered, gulped down a coffee, and then taken the train to central London. The commute from their house to his investment bank took just over an hour—in good times. With the constant delays and overcrowded trains, it often took ninety minutes before he arrived at his glass office tower in Canary Wharf.

Eva sighed softly. David had been working even more since the economic crisis of 2023. During the week, they hardly saw each other. He usually came home after 10 PM, when the children were already asleep, silently ate his reheated dinner, and then collapsed in front of the television until Eva gently guided him to bed. She cherished the weekends and the rare vacations all the more, when they came together again as a real family.

The coffee machine's humming stopped. Eva took the steaming pot and poured herself a cup. The intense aroma of freshly ground coffee filled the small but cozy kitchen with its light blue cabinets and worn oak countertop.

The door hinges squeaked softly as her sixteen-year-old daughter Emma entered the kitchen. She had already packed her school bag—a backpack decorated with buttons and patches—which she carelessly dropped onto one of the empty chairs. Emma wore dark jeans and a burgundy sweater that contrasted with her chestnut brown hair, which, unlike her mother's, she wore cut short. Her eyes—the exact green of her father's—looked tired and slightly annoyed at the world, typical for her age.

"Emma, could you please turn on the television?" Eva asked as she carefully flipped the fried eggs with a wooden spatula.

Emma groaned softly but complied with her mother's request. She stood up, shuffled to the flat screen mounted on the cream-colored kitchen wall, and turned it on. With the remote in hand, she dropped back onto the chair and selected the American news channel NUW News. She turned up the volume.

On the screen appeared the familiar face of Professor Arthur Waterstone, who was introduced as a Russia expert. His gray blow-dried hairstyle and rimless glasses had become his trademark. The presenter, a blonde woman in a bright red suit, leaned forward with a serious expression.

"Professor Waterstone, you're talking about a disturbing pattern in the Russian president's actions. Could you explain that for our viewers?"

The professor nodded significantly and looked directly into the camera. His voice was firm and authoritative as he answered: "The Russian president loves such number games. We remember: On 8.8.2008, Russian troops invaded Georgia. Two days after the Olympic Games in Beijing, we had 2.22.2022, and two days later, on 2.24.2022, he invaded Ukraine."

He leaned forward, his eyes flashing behind his glasses. "And we remember the second of March of the same year, when there was a strange incident—a message from Russia to NATO, I suspect. Two NATO military aircraft disappeared near Ukraine, just one hundred kilometers from the border, suddenly vanishing from radar. A fighter jet and shortly afterward a rescue helicopter that was sent to search for the pilot. To this day, NATO remains silent about it. The reason for the two crashes on March 2, 2022, is still unknown to the public."

The presenter raised a perfectly plucked eyebrow. "And Professor Waterstone, you suspect that Russia is planning World War Three for 11.22.2025." Her voice carried a barely concealed undertone of skepticism, almost amusement.

The professor turned briefly to her, then back to the camera. His face was stony as he answered with a firm voice: "Yes, or three days before that, on 11.19.2025."

Eva yawned with boredom and rolled her eyes. She had heard Waterstone's theories many times before. The professor with his conspiracy ideas had become a sort of regular guest on news broadcasts in recent years. He had already prophesied the same for 11.22.2024 or 11.19.2024 —and nothing had happened.

She glanced at Emma, who was staring at the screen with an empty gaze, absentmindedly twirling a strand of her hair. Eva knew that her daughter was also familiar with the professor's theory. 911 as the American emergency number, 112 as the European one—both united in today's date: 11.19.2025.

Waterstone was just explaining his theory of connections with increasingly excited voice. How before the Ukraine war, the German Chancellor had traveled to Russia, and on the day of his return, there had been a widespread failure of German police emergency numbers. Or how on 11.11.2021, when the Russian troop buildup was already in full swing, both emergency numbers had failed nationwide in many German states.

"The date 11.19.2025 combines both emergency numbers," Waterstone emphasized with a grave voice. "The 911 and the 112."

Waterstone continued, his index finger raised in the air: "The Russian president hates the Bilderbergers—a powerful, influential secret society that emerged from the Freemasons. The founding of this society is connected to the 111th day of the year 1944, when American troops crossed the Rhine. Parts of the 110th and 112th Infantry Division were transferred to Heidelberg according to my theory because of influential Freemasons who loved numerology. From this merger later emerged that influential secret society—the Bilderbergers, who later established Germany's emergency number."

The professor gestured energetically, his eyes bright with fervor. "In 1948, these numbers were used regionally and became nationally valid in 1973. And decades later, thanks to the Bilderbergers' influence, 112 became the European emergency number. Since 2.11.1991, 112 is not only the German but the European emergency number, similar to 911 in the USA. And the date 11.19.2025 contains both emergency numbers."

Eva stirred mechanically in the pan while half-listening. The professor's theories were becoming increasingly far-fetched.

"Particularly interesting is 2.11.2025 *(europeans write it 11.2.2025, first day, then month),* the European Emergency Number Day, which was chosen because 2/11 reminds of the emergency number. On this day, a Russian bomber coming from the Kaliningrad enclave seemingly strayed from its course and flew exactly 1 minute and 12 seconds over NATO territory—another wink at the Bilderbergers, including the US President, who has been one of them since 2010. 'Strayed from course'—a wordplay with Kursk, the contested Russian region."

A small graphic was displayed on the screen,

highlighting the two emergency numbers in the date: 1**9.11.2**025 for 911 and 19.11.2025 for 112.

"That numbers and dates are played with is also official," Waterstone continued, pointing at the graphic with a pen. "For instance, 2/11 has officially been the European Emergency Number Day since 2009 because the date contains the emergency number. It's an action day created by the EU Commission and EU Parliament."

He cursed slightly as the presenter obviously tried to suppress a laugh. "This happens to me often," he muttered, "even when the facts are obvious. After all, I didn't make up that the EU Commission plays with dates and numbers—that's official and not one of my theories."

Eva placed the plate with fried eggs in front of Emma on the table. "Here, darling. Eat before it gets cold."

Emma nodded absentmindedly, her gaze still fixed on the television, where Waterstone was now diving into another explanatory loop.

"That the Russian president hates the Bilderbergers is widely known," the professor continued, his index finger raised warningly. "According to my theory—and I know many find it absurd—the Bilderbergers, who emerged from the numerology-loving secret society of Freemasons, also love number games. For the founding of their secret society, they simply reversed the year 1945 for the end of the war. 45 became 54. Just as George Orwell did for his book '1984'—he reversed the year 1948. And so 1954 became the official founding year of the Bilderbergers, who probably strive for a dystopian world, as Orwell described it, with a permanent conflict against a great enemy."

The professor pulled a crumpled notebook from his jacket pocket and hastily flipped through it. "I suspect that part of the Freemasons had the idea for their secret society for some time and had been planning it. This secret society played its connections and chose Heidelberg for the relocation of the 110th and 112th Infantry Division. The reason lies in the Heidel**berger Bilder**handschrift manuscript of the Sachenspiegel, an old feudal law book from the Middle Ages."

His eyes glowed feverishly as he delved deeper into his theory. "If you reverse the word components 'Heidel**berger Bilder**berger manuscript' , you get their name: 'Bilder Berger'. One founding member, by the way, was a member of the Reiter-SS. The reason that it was parts of the 110th and 112th Division was that the day when US troops crossed the Rhine was the 111th day. The Bilderbergers exerted their influence, and that led to the two German emergency numbers years later. Decades later, the Bilderbergers even managed to standardize the European emergency number as 112."

Eva was now expertly mixing the batter for pancakes—a mixture of flour, eggs, milk, and a pinch of salt. While stirring the ingredients, she kept glancing skeptically at the television.

"According to my theory, the Bilderbergers aim to rule through emergency laws," Waterstone continued, his voice now more subdued, almost conspiratorial. "They already tried it during the pandemic in some European countries like France, but public pressure was too strong. Some also suspect that the Bilderbergers sow terror to take away civil rights from their own citizens."

He took a sip of water from a glass beside him. "The Bilderberger secret society consists of media moguls, heads of government—including US presidents and chancellors and other European government leaders—military personnel, and business bosses who have enormous influence. Many believe that the Bilderbergers are striving for world domination and trying to restrict civil rights more and more."

The presenter cleared her throat, obviously trying to steer the conversation in another direction. "Professor, what do you think, why does the Russian president engage in such number games?"

Waterstone rolled his eyes so obviously that even Emma laughed briefly. Hadn't the woman been listening? He took a deep breath and gave a slight sigh.

"Well, I think it's also a wink at the numerology-loving Bilderbergers, whom he hates so much. I think he wants to annoy them by putting on such a number show."

"Professor, what do you think the Bilderbergers are planning?" The presenter tried to structure the conversation. "You mentioned an Orwellian state?"

"The Bilderbergers are trying to build a kind of Orwellian state and have been planning it for decades," Waterstone answered emphatically. "Step by step, they are expanding it and use every opportunity that presents itself, such as terrorist attacks and pandemics, to further erode civil rights. I'm sure of that."

He leaned forward, his voice becoming more urgent. "Here in the West, they don't have it easy, but we repeatedly see how civil rights are curtailed, laws are deliberately complicated to create more arbitrariness. The press in some Western countries has already been muzzled. Out of fear of lawsuits, they report in line with the government."

Waterstone gestured with his hands, his face reddened with fervor. "Even during the pandemic, some governments tried to rule with emergency laws, but the pressure from the population was, thank God, too strong. Especially in Europe, we have very bad conditions where governments make laws at the European level and then just have them rubber-stamped by the national parliaments. Then they say it's the pressure from Brussels, what can we do about it?"

His voice grew quieter, almost a whisper, as if he wanted to reveal a terrible secret. "For many unnoticed, the death penalty for insurgencies was also rushed through the national parliaments via the EU. This was done with the Lisbon Treaties. The explanations included there explicitly allow the reintroduction of the death penalty in case of war or imminent danger of war. They also allow the killing of people to suppress a rebellion or riot."

The presenter seemed troubled and tried to bring the conversation back to firmer ground. "You say you've deciphered the Bilderbergers' secret messaging system. Can you tell us more about that?"

Waterstone's eyes lit up. He was now completely in his element. "That's right. You see, the Bilderbergers got their name from a hotel of one of the founding members. In 'hotel' is 'tel', like telephone. They didn't want to use a telephone, but hotels. But even there, they often can't speak openly, and so they've created a messaging system where you can read their plans from the locations and names of the hotels."

He flipped hastily through his notebook. "I searched and found: Bretton Woods, Chernobyl, 'Grave around Denmark' plan, where we can already see how some Bilderbergers are putting pressure on Denmark to give up Greenland. Even a war of EU states against the USA seems possible, which would explain the grave plan. And their newest plan, which is just becoming readable and might take a few more years: a supervirus that kills off almost all people, a plague or something like that. A bioweapon."

"That's terrible," exclaimed the presenter, who now seemed fascinated.

"Yes, that's just how the Bilderbergers are. Wars are normal for them." Waterstone shrugged as if he were talking about the weather.

"Let's start with Chernobyl," he continued, his voice now calmer, more factual. "In 1965, around the time the reactor was being planned, they met in Cernobbio. With a bit of imagination—after all, it's not so easy to find a hotel with such an exact name, and what hotel calls itself Grave, though Grove is similar enough, but I assume they also founded one or two hotels—the name also reminds of Nobel's CERN, which we know, the Large Hydrogen Collider. Agents probably knew where the Soviets were planning the reactor, which is why they could incorporate it into their meeting place."

He lowered his voice to a whisper. "Presumably, agents installed a defective part that then malfunctioned as desired on the day they wanted it to, triggering the meltdown. That was exactly in the middle of their meeting from April 25-27, 1986, on April 26, when they met in the **UK** for

'**UK**raine', at the Gleneagle Hotel for 'Clean Eagle'. The following year, they met again in Cernobbio—the only two times in 70 years."

The presenter cast a nervous glance toward the control room, but Waterstone couldn't be stopped.

"Now let's move on to Bretton Woods. The USA was in the Vietnam War at that time, and money was running out. The gold standard of Bretton Woods prevented high indebtedness. Nixon, a Bilderberger, urgently needed a source of money. In 1970 they met at the Hotel Quellenhof—for 'money source hope' (in german Geld**quelle hof**fen). In 1971 in Woodstock—for Bretton Woods, which also contains a 'Woods'. That was in April, a few months after the meeting Nixon began to withdraw from the Bretton Woods gold standard. The dollar was no longer convertible into gold. The currency became something based only on trust and was no longer backed by gold."

His eyes widened as he elaborated on his thoughts. "The Bilderbergers knew that in a few decades their monetary system would collapse, so they also prepared for a major war that would then be needed. They knew that eventually the banks would become unsound and could break, the national debts so high that their system could collapse. In 1972 they met at La Reserve du Knokke Heist, alluding to Fort Knox, where the gold reserves were stored. The Bilderbergers often meet in hotels whose names allude to kings and

Caesars."

He flipped further in his notebook. "In 2013, another of their plans started. They met at the Grove Hotel, whose name reminds of 'Grave'. And 'Grave' where? The answer came at the next hotel, 2014, where they met in Denmark in Copenhagen. 'Grave' and 'Denmark'. We could already see the beginnings of the planning in 2016 when the Bilderberger president began to publicly express his interest in Greenland, which belongs to Denmark. And we've seen that more and more aggressively lately."

His voice became even more intense as he came to the last part of his revelations. "Then there's the plan that's starting in recent years—the pandemic. In 2021 they met at Geneve Lake—'Geneva' reminds of 'Gene Eva', Adam and Eve. In 2022 at the Mandarin Oriental Hotel, then in 2023 at the **PESTo**na Hotel in Portugal. 'Pest' in the name! Pest is the german word for plague. Before that at the China Hotel, 'Mandarin Oriental', Covid came from China, after all. And what else fits? Right, the Spanish flu! That was 2024, Royal Palace Hotel in Madrid. So the Pest hotel between the China-reminiscent Mandarin Oriental and the Royal Palace in Spain. Alluding to two of the most devastating pandemics: Covid from China and the Spanish Flu."

A graphic was displayed:

2021 at Geneva Lake — for Gene Eva — Adam and

Eve (Eva is german for Eve)

2022 at Mandarin Oriental — for China and Covid

2023 at the **PEST**ona Hotel in Portugal (Pest the german word for plague. Bilderberger is a german name and means translated Picture Mountain)

2024 at the Royal Palace Hotel in Madrid, Spain — Symbolically for Spanish Flu

His hands trembled with excitement. "Additionally, in 2023 there was also 'Mall' in the name, which reminds of 'Mail'. The meeting in May 2023 at Pestana was in Portugal, which reminds of 'Porto' (Porto a german world for stamp on letter). Perhaps a hint to send a pathogen by mail. It seems to be a very bad virus, because of the reference to Adam and Eve, where virtually all populations are supposed to die, and the Bilderbergers can then rebuild the population undisturbed, residing in the palaces of the extinct world. And they have already begun to weaken the WHO for their plan. The USA has already withdrawn from the WHO."

"That's terrible," repeated the presenter, now visibly disturbed.

Eva shook her head and turned to Emma: "Can you please switch to another news channel?"

Emma took the remote and zapped up a few programs to another news channel. On the screen now appeared shocking images: An apartment block was in flames, black smoke rising into the gray sky. Firefighters fought desperately against the inferno, while paramedics transported injured people on stretchers to waiting ambulances.

The news anchor reported with a serious voice: "Last night, a Russian missile missed its target and hit a Polish city. Something that also happened during the Syrian war, where Russian missiles missed their target and hit Iran. There were numerous fatalities. An apartment block is in flames. There were four deaths and thirty-seven injured. The Russian Defense Ministry says it was an accident. It was not their intention to hit a target in Poland."

The camera panned over the debris, showing weeping residents desperately searching for relatives. "However, the Russian Defense Minister repeatedly emphasized that the NATO eastern expansion, which has been happening since 1997, should be reversed. Russia also bombed energy networks in Ukraine again. The American President threatened sanctions and tariffs in response."

The image changed to footage from Washington. "At the same time, the US President announced that he would increase military aid to Ukraine by another 1.5 billion US dollars. To be delivered once again are long-range missiles for the HIMARS system, which can hit targets 300 kilometers away. Plus another 1000 Javelin anti-tank missiles, 80 Harpoon anti-ship missiles, 40 Bradley infantry fighting vehicles, drones, and ammunition."

The anchor in the studio suddenly looked up and touched his ear, obviously receiving new information through his earpiece. "We've just received the news that the Russian President's address, announced for today, is being broadcast on Russian television."

The address was connected. The image showed the Russian President behind a massive desk of dark wood. The Russian flag stood to his right, the state emblems emblazoned on the wood-paneled wall behind him. His face looked serious, almost grim, as he looked into the camera.

"Dear fellow citizens," he began, his voice calm and controlled, yet with an undertone of suppressed anger. "The aggressive behavior of the West has severely damaged our economy. Despite all our efforts, the West was not willing to lift the sanctions. It is the West that, with its hostile, aggressive, Russophobic behavior, is trying to destroy our country, which we love so much. I have often emphasized that these sanctions constitute an act of war. The weapons deliveries to Ukraine also represent a form of hybrid warfare."

The Russian President slammed his flat hand on the table, an unexpected gesture of frustration. "We bomb what we deem necessary. To the Americans' threat to impose further sanctions and tariffs on us, we now counter with this: I threaten the West with war if they do not lift the sanctions against our country by 2 p.m. today."

Emma sat at the table and poked listlessly at her scrambled eggs with her fork while listening to the news. Like everyone else, she was concerned. The pandemic, which once dominated the news broadcasts, was almost forgotten after another wave of a mutated strain had swept across the world last winter, against which the vaccines didn't offer particularly good protection. But that too had subsided. Now it was the tensions between the West and Russia that weren't abating but had reached a new level of escalation.

Her mother came to the oak wood table with the heavy cast-iron pan and heaped a generous portion of slightly browned fried potatoes onto her plate with the worn wooden cooking spoon, whose handle was already shiny from years of use. The smell of fried garlic and onions rose to Emma's nose but couldn't dampen her growing unease.

"Thank you," she murmured, thanking her mother. Then she raised her gaze and looked Eva directly in the eyes. "Do you think there will be nuclear war?" she asked, her voice quieter than usual, as if uttering the words could conjure the calamity.

Eva tried to smile reassuringly, but the fine line between her eyebrows betrayed her own concern. "I hope not. The Russians surely won't start a nuclear war. They're just threatening with it," she answered with a conviction she didn't feel herself.

But inwardly, she didn't believe her own words.

Emma also noticed that her mother hadn't said what she really thought, but was only trying to reassure her. She sighed heavily and put her fork down beside her plate, her appetite gone.

CHAPTER 2: THE WORLD ON THE BRINK

On the television, the image switched to a live broadcast from Washington D.C. A fanfare sounded, and the seal of the White House appeared on the screen. The news anchor announced that the US President would hold a press conference in the James S. Brady Press Briefing Room of the White House.

The small, rectangular room with its blue walls and distinctive podium was filled to capacity. The forty seats reserved for accredited media representatives of the White House Press Corps were barely enough; more journalists crowded against the side walls. The air in the overcrowded room was stuffy, the tension almost palpable.

With a serious expression, the US President entered the room. He wore an impeccably tailored dark blue suit with a burgundy tie. His face looked tense, the lines around his eyes and mouth deeper than usual. With measured steps, he walked to the podium, which bore the presidential seal. The flashes of the photographers filled the room with brief, harsh bursts of light.

The President laid his notes on the podium, gripped the edges, and looked firmly into the cameras. "My fellow Americans, friends around the world," he began, his voice firm and determined. "This morning, the Russian President issued an unacceptable threat against the United States and our allies. He demands the immediate lifting of all sanctions imposed as a result of Russia's ongoing illegal aggression against Ukraine."

He paused briefly, his knuckles turning white as he gripped the podium more firmly. "I will not withdraw the sanctions imposed against Russia. In fact, we will impose even more sanctions and even tariffs if Russia continues to bomb energy facilities, which violates our agreement. I will also increase military aid to Ukraine, as already announced, by another 1.5 billion US dollars."

Eva and Emma exchanged horrified glances. The mere thought that both sides were not backing down but further intensifying the situation sent a cold shiver down Eva's spine.

"Yes, I heard it," Eva said with a choked voice. A strange feeling spread through her, as if she were standing on the edge of an abyss and could feel the bottomless chasm beneath her. A feeling of the imminent end of the world. "You'd better stay here today. Don't go to school," she said worriedly to her daughter.

A surprised smile flashed across Emma's tense face. "Okay. Should I wake Tim?" she asked, somehow relieved that her mother herself suggested skipping school—something that would have been unthinkable in normal times.

Tim was her little brother, only seven years old. Eva imagined his sleeping face, peaceful and unconcerned, the blonde curls wildly distributed on the pillow, unaware of the looming danger. "No. Let him sleep," she decided. The longer he could stay in his innocent world, the better.

On the screen, the press conference had broken into full chaos. Reporters had jumped up, shouting over each other and stretching their microphones forward. "Mr. President! Mr. President!" One of the journalists had asked what the new sanctions would entail.

The President raised his hand to calm the crowd. "We will exclude more Russian banks from SWIFT. Additionally, further measures will be decided, which we will announce in the coming days. Including very high tariffs. We will coordinate with our alliance partners on this."

SWIFT—the international system by which banks reconcile financial transactions with each other—was the financial backbone of the global economy. Exclusion from it was tantamount to economic execution.

The President couldn't continue speaking but was interrupted by the reporters. A young man with wild curly hair and thick-framed glasses jumped up. "Mr. President! Mr. President!" he called, wildly gesticulating with his arms. He had jumped up like most other reporters and was trying to make himself heard loudly.

The President, who was just supporting himself with both arms on the podium, looked at him and nodded slightly. "Yes, please," he said, looking at the reporter.

"Are you prepared to risk a war with Russia for this?" asked the reporter, barely concealing the consternation in his voice. "The Russian President openly threatened war this morning in case the existing sanctions are not withdrawn—and you're saying there will now be even more new sanctions!"

The President took a deep breath. The tension was clearly visible to him as he adjusted his glasses with a trembling finger. He took a sip from the water glass on the podium and then said with a controlled voice: "I don't want to elaborate on your question, but just say this much: If Russia wants to risk a war, we will be ready with the necessary determination and with all means available to us, even to the extreme, to defend our country and our allies with all means at our disposal. We will not start the war, but we will defend ourselves if it should come to war."

A shocked murmur went through the room. The US President had de facto declared war on Russia, since the Russian President had already announced this morning that war would come if the sanctions were not withdrawn.

Eva felt her heart racing. She stood up and went to the window. Outside was a completely normal Tuesday morning in a London suburb. Women pushed strollers, businesspeople hurried to their cars with briefcases, a postman cycled along the street. No one seemed to realize that they might be experiencing their last hours in a world of peace.

"We should call David," Emma suddenly said. Her voice sounded unusually thin and anxious.

Eva nodded and reached for her mobile phone. With trembling fingers, she dialed her husband's number, but she only reached the mailbox. She tried again, with the same result. "He must be in a meeting," she murmured, more to herself than to Emma. "Or the lines are overloaded."

She sent him a text message: "Call me immediately. It's important. Love you." Then she put the phone on the kitchen counter and stared at it, as if she could make it ring through sheer willpower.

Emma had turned off the television. The uninterrupted news about the impending catastrophe became too much. She now sat silently at the table, her slender fingers nervously playing with the hem of her burgundy sweater.

The silence in the room was suddenly interrupted by loud pounding at the front door. Both jumped. Eva hurried to the door, Emma close behind her.

CHAPTER 3: THE ESCAPE

When Eva opened the door, David Thompson stood in the entrance, his face flushed and sweaty, as if he had been running. He was about 6'1" tall and very slim, almost wiry. His once thick, chestnut brown hair already showed first gray streaks at the temples, and the deep lines around his green eyes testified to the hardships of recent years. He wore an elegant black suit, an immaculate white shirt, and a sapphire blue tie, which was now slightly loosened. In his right hand, he held a worn brown leather briefcase, which he almost threw onto the table as he stormed into the house.

"Darling, we have to leave," he said breathlessly, gasping for air. He tried to control his panic, but his wide-open eyes betrayed his fear.

"What's going on, sweetheart?" asked Eva, though she already guessed the answer. Part of her wondered about her own question—as if she hadn't spent the last few hours in growing horror in front of the television. Was it because the situation seemed so surreal? She didn't know.

David hastily took off his expensive designer jacket and carelessly threw it over a chair—another sign of his extraordinary agitation. He was normally meticulously neat, especially with his expensive clothing.

"We need to get out of the city. Into the countryside. There's going to be war soon. Everyone's already talking about it," he explained hastily, while loosening his tie. "I've seen the first stores being emptied. People are shopping like crazy, the shelves are already half empty. Quick, pack your things. Take only the essentials. And pack food too."

His agitation was contagious. Eva felt her heart beating faster, her palms becoming moist. The abstract danger she had felt while watching television transformed into tangible panic.

"Emma, go wake Tim," Eva said to her daughter, who stood frozen in the doorway. "But don't scare him. Tell him we're going on a trip, a surprise trip."

Emma nodded silently and hurried up the stairs to her little brother's room. She burst through the door decorated with superhero stickers and called: "Tim, wake up!"

The little boy, who lay under his spaceship bedcover, opened his eyes sleepily. At seven years old, he was a miniature version of his father—the same green eyes, the same unruly hair, only in a lighter blond tone that he had inherited from his maternal grandmother.

"What is it?" mumbled Tim, who was still completely asleep and rubbing his eyes with small fists. He wore dinosaur-patterned pajamas that were already a bit too small—his ankles showed beneath the pants legs.

"We need to pack our things. Quick, get dressed," Emma urged, as she hurried to the wardrobe and yanked open the door.

She ran out of the room and got a large, navy blue hard-shell suitcase from the storage room, whose door squeaked as she hastily opened it. With the heavy suitcase, she ran back to Tim's room, where the boy still stood in his pajamas, confused and disoriented.

Emma threw the suitcase on the floor near his wardrobe and opened it frantically. The lid slammed back with a loud bang. "Why aren't you dressed yet?" she asked irritably, her nerves stretched to the breaking point.

"Why the hurry?" asked Tim, still not quite with it and confused by the sudden commotion.

Emma hesitated. How much should she tell her little brother? "There's going to be war soon. We have to get away from here," she finally explained, while trying to keep her voice calm.

Tim's eyes widened in shock. "War? Like on TV? With bombs and stuff?"

"Yes, with bombs," Emma confirmed quietly. "Come on, get dressed now," she added emphatically.

Tim began to dress hastily, now finally understanding the urgency of the situation. He put on jeans and a green sweater, while Emma pulled drawers out of the wardrobe and randomly threw clothing items into the suitcase: T-shirts, sweaters, socks, underwear—all jumbled together.

In the kitchen, David was busy packing food. He had fetched several sturdy cardboard boxes from the garage, in which Christmas decorations or old books were usually stored. Methodically, he emptied the pantry cupboards, throwing canned goods, pasta, rice, and preserved foods into the boxes.

A jar of pickled cucumbers slipped from his damp hands and shattered on the stone floor. Glass shards and pickles spread in a sticky puddle.

David cursed softly. Eva, who noticed the mishap, said, "Leave it. I'll clean it up." She reached for a cloth hanging over the tap.

"No, leave it. We don't have time," David replied in a sharp tone that was so unlike him. He looked aghast at Eva, who blushed slightly at his harsh response. It was habit and reflex that she wanted to clean up—an attempt to maintain a piece of normalcy in this chaotic situation.

"But it's going to stink. It's vinegar," Eva protested

weakly, while still putting the cloth back, inwardly still hoping that they might return later to clean up the mess.

David looked at her penetratingly, his eyes dark with worry. "It doesn't matter. Soon London might not exist anymore," he said in a quiet but urgent voice, to make his wife realize the seriousness of the situation.

Despite his words, Eva took a plastic bucket from under the sink, knelt down, and began collecting the shards and pickles. The sour liquid seeped into the grooves between the tiles, and the penetrating smell of vinegar and spices filled the air.

David suppressed a curse but let her continue. He had no time to argue. "Where did you store the long-lasting food? I bought some for the pandemic once," he asked, while putting more supplies into the boxes: flour, sugar, salt, oats—anything that would keep for a long time.

Eva looked up from her cleaning task. "Those? Oh, I put them in the basement. On the big shelves to the left of the washing machine."

David grabbed the first full box and carried it outside to their SUV, a robust Land Rover Defender in olive green, which he had bought used two years ago. It was an older model, built like a tank, with high ground clearance and four-wheel drive—perfect for the rough English countryside, but also for city traversal during floods, which had become increasingly common in recent years.

He opened the tailgate and pushed the box in, then hurried back into the house and down the steep basement stairs. In the damp, cold basement, which smelled of laundry detergent and old books, he found the nine large boxes of emergency supplies: cans of stew, freeze-dried meals, energy bars, water filters, and other survival equipment that he had acquired during the worst phase of the pandemic. Back then, his colleagues had laughed at him—now this foresight could save their lives.

David carried all nine boxes up one by one and stowed them in the SUV, which became fuller with each trip. Sweat streamed down his face and back, his expensive shirt clung to his skin, but he ignored the discomfort.

His wife Eva had meanwhile packed several suitcases with clothing and brought these down as well. "There are more suitcases upstairs in the bedroom," she said to David when they met in the hallway.

He glanced at the already full trunk of the Land Rover. "Well, we can fit a few more things in," he said and ran up the stairs to the bedroom. There he saw the packed suitcases—two medium-sized trolleys in burgundy, which they had bought during their last vacation together in Cornwall. He grabbed both by the handles and hurried back down the narrow stairs.

On the steep wooden staircase, he almost stumbled when his right foot slipped. "Don't break your neck now," he cursed and reluctantly slowed his pace for the rest of the descent.

Emma and Tim came from the children's room. Tim wore a small green dinosaur-patterned backpack, into which he had hastily stuffed his favorite toys: a worn teddy bear, a few action figures, and his favorite book about dinosaurs. Emma had two suitcases in hand—one for herself and one with Tim's clothes.

"There's still a suitcase upstairs," she said to her father, then cursed softly when she saw the already full car.

"Is there anything important in it?" asked David, while trying to stow the two trolleys in the trunk by squeezing them between the boxes.

Emma hesitated. "Uh, some of my favorite dresses. So yes, important," she answered, knowing that her father might decide to leave the suitcase behind if she gave a different answer.

"All right, I'll get it," said David and ran upstairs again. He found the pink suitcase, which was overflowing with Emma's clothes, and dragged it downstairs. With some effort, he managed to squeeze this last suitcase into the packed trunk. He closed the tailgate with a determined bang.

They were already sitting in the SUV, the engines running, and David was about to drive off when he suddenly remembered something.

"Did you load the camping gear into the car?"

Eva slapped her forehead with the palm of her hand. "No. Forgot," she cursed.

Both got out, while Tim and Emma remained seated in the car, as David and Eva hurried to the garage. The small, detached garage was crammed with gardening tools, bicycles, and camping equipment from better times. They pulled out a large family tent, four sleeping bags, sleeping pads, and other gear: a camping stove with gas cartridge, folding chairs, and a small folding table.

They stowed the equipment in the Land Rover, partly on the back seat between Tim and Emma, who had to squeeze together. The tent, a dome model in bright orange, was placed on top of the suitcases in the trunk.

David remembered something else. "I still have the four full 20-liter gas canisters that I got for the pandemic," he said and went back to the garage.

The heavy metal canisters stood in a corner, each with a red warning sticker. David lifted the first one—his back protested against the weight—and carried it to the car. With some pushing and shoving, he got the first canister into the trunk.

Looking at the overstuffed storage space, he realized that not all canisters would fit. He saw one of his own suitcases, an old brown leather suitcase that he had inherited from his father. Resolutely, he pulled it out and threw it towards the front door. "That stays here," he muttered. Clothes could be replaced; gasoline in a post-nuclear world would be priceless.

He stowed the other three gas canisters in the SUV, each at a strategic point to distribute the weight, and then slammed the tailgate. The car was now packed to the roof, the suspension noticeably lower than normal.

David got back into the car, and they drove off. As they drove along the street, they saw that they weren't the only ones fleeing. Several of their neighbors were also frantically packing and loading their cars. Screams and crying children's voices emanated from some houses. An elderly woman stood bewildered in her front yard, unsure what to do.

David drove slowly, also to see what their neighbors were doing. He turned on the radio, and immediately the tense voices of news anchors filled the car.

"Russia has issued an ultimatum to the US. They have one hour to withdraw the sanctions," announced a female voice with an attempt at an objective tone. "It has also been reported that stock markets in Russia have collapsed. There are bank runs in Moscow and St. Petersburg. Similar scenes of financial chaos are being reported from financial centers worldwide. The stock exchanges in New York, London, and Tokyo have suspended trading after the indices fell by more than 20 percent within minutes."

After they had left their residential area with its well-maintained row houses and small front gardens behind, David accelerated as quickly as the heavy traffic allowed. He repeatedly exceeded the speed limit when a gap opened up. The danger of getting caught speeding was the last thing that concerned him now.

Near the entrance to the M25 motorway, the large ring road around London, was a larger gas station. David glanced at the fuel gauge of his Land Rover. The tank was only half full—too little for an escape into the unknown.

He slowed down and approached the gas station. It was busy, but not yet so crowded that one had to wait long. There were no looters at work yet, but the lines at the pumps were already worryingly long.

David put on the turn signal and pulled into the gas station. "You go in and see if they still have gas canisters. If they do, buy some," he said to his wife.

He stopped at a free pump and watched the man at the neighboring pump who was busy filling several gas canisters. All around them, he saw the same picture: people not only fueling their vehicles but also filling every available container with the precious fuel.

Eva got out and went into the gas station, whose

brightly lit sales area was already full of people. She weaved her way through the crowd; the shelves were already half empty. Canned goods, water, batteries—anything that might be useful in a crisis was largely gone. On a shelf, she discovered two 30-liter gas canisters made of red plastic. Without hesitation, she took both and made her way to the checkout, where a long line had already formed.

The tension in the room was palpable. An older woman was quietly weeping as she placed her purchases on the conveyor belt—mainly baby food and diapers, probably for grandchildren. A bearded man in work clothes was arguing heatedly with another customer about the possible range of Russian nuclear missiles. Others stood silently, their faces pale and expressionless, as if in shock.

Eva waited patiently, paid for the canisters, and hurried back to the car, where David had finished fueling and was standing next to the vehicle. He took the heavy canisters from her.

"Go queue up to pay," David said to his wife, while hastily opening the cap of the first canister and inserting the pump nozzle. The gasoline flowed with a steady rushing sound into the container, the smell of fuel rose to Eva's nose as she headed back toward the gas station.

She waited in the queue, which stretched outside, and glanced nervously at the watch on her wrist. 9:45 a.m. Still a good four hours until the ultimatum expired. Would this time be enough to get out of the city and find a safe place?

When she finally got her turn, she put the money for the gasoline on the counter. The cashier, a young woman with tired eyes and trembling hands, took it and wordlessly handed her the receipt. Eva nodded gratefully and hurried back to the car.

David had meanwhile filled both canisters and safely stowed them in the vehicle. He was already sitting at the wheel, the engine running. As soon as Eva got in, he drove off.

As they reached the exit of the gas station and wanted to return to the road, a government convoy was just passing by. Several black limousines with tinted windows, accompanied by police motorcycles with flashing blue lights, raced along the road. The elegant cars with British flags on the fenders moved like a dark snake through the increasingly dense traffic.

"They're headed to the airport," Eva remarked as she saw the convoy turning onto the highway entrance that led to Heathrow Airport.

"Yes, they're probably fleeing," David replied grimly, while waiting for a gap in the traffic to get onto the road.

He finally managed to merge into the traffic, and they drove toward the M25. The highway entrance was already congested, but they moved forward slowly. The lanes toward London were almost empty, while in the opposite direction—out of the city—vehicles crowded bumper to bumper.

Tim pressed his pale face against the side window and observed the passing landscape with wide eyes. "Where are we going, Daddy?" he asked in a quiet voice.

David cast a quick glance in the rearview mirror and forced himself to a reassuring smile. "We're going to Uncle Ben's, on the coast. It will be like a little vacation," he answered, trying to make his voice sound calm.

"But I forgot my Nintendo," Tim protested.

"That doesn't matter," Emma chimed in, taking his hand. "We can play other games. Card games or something."

The journey on the highway was arduous. Again and again the traffic stalled, then flowed again for a short stretch before coming to a standstill again. The drivers became increasingly aggressive, honking and cutting each other off. Several times they saw cars standing by the roadside with open hoods or flat tires—victims of haste and overload.

On the radio, special announcements alternated with hectic analyses. Experts were brought in to discuss the probability of a nuclear conflict, while reporters from capitals around the world reported on mass panic, looting, and overwhelmed emergency services.

CHAPTER 4: DESTINATION PARIS

Flight AF4011 from New York to Paris.

An A380 of a French airline was just taking off from John F. Kennedy Airport in New York. The massive machine, a double-decker giant with a wingspan of almost eighty meters, rolled majestically to the runway. Its white paintwork gleamed in the sunlight, the blue-white-red logo of the airline proudly emblazoned on the tail fin. Weighing over 560 tons, the A380 was the largest passenger aircraft in the world—a flying palace that could carry over 500 passengers.

The destination was Paris, the City of Lights, the City of Love.

In economy class, about half of the seats were occupied. The padded seats in soft blue were comfortable, if not spacious, with small screens on each backrest and narrow trays that could be folded out from the armrests.

The 54-year-old Sandra Hopkins and her 57-year-old husband Thomas were on a vacation flight to France. They sat in the middle of the cabin, Sandra by the window, Thomas in the middle seat. Both were well-groomed and conservatively dressed—she in a navy blue blouse and pearl gray pants, he in a checked shirt and beige chinos. Their silver-gray hair and the wrinkles around their eyes testified to a long, fulfilled life.

It was their thirtieth wedding anniversary, which they wanted to spend in the most romantic city in the world. They had planned months in advance, had studied travel guides and memorized French vocabulary. Sandra had a small notebook in which she had listed all the sights they wanted to visit.

They planned to see this steel colossus, the Eiffel Tower, which had once been built in Paris at the end of the 19th century for the World's Fair, and about which many Parisians at the time complained because they thought it ruined the cityscape. It was originally planned to dismantle the Eiffel Tower after the World's Fair, but it was left standing. Over time, it had become the symbol of the French capital, an iron landmark that every visitor had to see.

Lovers from all over the world felt magically attracted to that steel colossus, held together by millions of rivets. With its curved shape, it somehow also reminded of a giant phallus, a monument of technical masculinity in a city of art and culture. It could not be missing from any vacation photo from Paris, its distinctive profile as unmistakable as a fingerprint.

Thomas had reserved a table months in advance at one of the exclusive restaurants on the first level of the tower, the "Le 58 Tour Eiffel," with its spectacular view over the Seine and the elegant boulevards. The reservation was worth a small fortune, but only the best for their thirtieth wedding anniversary.

The aircraft of flight AF4011 rolled to the runway, its weight making the ground vibrate beneath the massive wheels. The engines howled as the pilot increased power. The A380 accelerated and took off leisurely, the nose rising gently into the blue sky above New York. The passengers were pressed slightly into their seats by the acceleration forces, a light tingling in the stomach accompanying the ascent.

Sandra pressed her husband's right hand firmly. Her hand was wet with sweat, her fingers cramped. She was afraid and nervous. As always when flying. The taking off and landing were the worst moments for her, moments when she became aware of the fragility of her own life, of the thin line between existence and non-existence.

Lovingly, she looked at her husband, who answered her hand-squeezing with a warm smile. The thirty years together had left their marks—in the gray hair, the laugh lines around his eyes, the small scars and quirks that a life leaves behind. But in his blue eyes, she could still see the young man she had fallen in love with so many years ago.

"Don't be afraid. Nothing will happen," he said and looked at her with a loving smile, while gently stroking her hand. His voice was deep and reassuring, an anchor in the uncertainty of the moment.

The aircraft set course northward. The pilot executed a gentle curve, the wings tilted slightly, and the A380 aligned itself with its predetermined course. Via Greenland and Ireland, they would then head to France, a route that the gigantic aircraft would cover in about eight hours.

Sandra gradually relaxed as the ascent was completed and the plane reached its cruising altitude. The seatbelt signs went off with a soft 'ping', and the flight attendants began to serve drinks. Thomas ordered a whiskey for himself and a white wine for Sandra, to toast their wedding anniversary.

They clinked glasses, the glasses tinkling softly against each other. "To thirty wonderful years," said Thomas. "And to many more."

Sandra smiled and sipped her wine. She pulled a small photo album from her handbag, which she had prepared specifically for this trip. It contained pictures from their shared history—their wedding, the birth of their two children, vacation photos, Christmas celebrations, all the small and large moments that make up a life.

They leafed through the album together, laughed about old hairstyles and outdated fashions, became sentimental over pictures of their children, who were now grown and had their own families. It was a journey through time, a reminder of what they had experienced and achieved together.

As they reminisced, they were unaware that the political situation in Europe was escalating. That an ultimatum had been issued, which would soon expire. That the world, as they knew it, stood on the brink of the abyss.

The A380 continued to fly, majestic and undeterred, while beneath it the Atlantic glittered in the afternoon sun. The passengers ate, drank, watched movies, slept—all everyday activities in a world that would soon no longer exist.

Sandra eventually fell asleep, her head leaning against Thomas's shoulder, the photo album still on her lap. He looked at her sleeping face, the fine lines around her eyes and her mouth, which spoke of laughter and life, and felt a wave of affection. Thirty years—and he still loved her, perhaps even more than on their wedding day.

Outside, the sky slowly grew darker as they approached the east coast of Canada. The A380 flew at over 900 kilometers per hour through the thin, icy air at an altitude of 10,000 meters, unimpressed by the human dramas unfolding beneath it.

CHAPTER 5: THE ULTIMATUM

2 PM. November 17, 2025.

Time passed relentlessly. Second by second, minute by minute. In the Kremlin, the massive wall clock ticked with hypnotic precision, each click echoing through the magnificent hall like a heartbeat. The gold-decorated hands slowly but surely moved toward the decisive position.

The ultimatum expired.

The USA was not willing to withdraw its sanctions against Russia. Despite the clear threat, despite the international tensions, despite the pleas from numerous neutral countries for de-escalation—the American President had decided to stand firm. A decision that would seal the fate of the world.

In the capitals of the world, people held their breath. In the corridors of power, there was a silence that was louder than any scream. The first fourteen hours of the day had passed like in a flight, and yet everyone felt they had lived through an eternity. Diplomatic channels were glowing, desperate attempts were made to build a last bridge, to find a last compromise.

All in vain.

Shortly after the ultimatum expired, a small Russian bomber fleet took off from a Russian air force base near the Kaliningrad enclave, the former Königsberg. They broke through the gray clouds like a death angel descending from the sky.

The fleet consisted of two Tupolev Tu-160s, the pride of the Russian air force. Since the early eighties, those bombers had been in service, first under the flag of the Soviet Union, later Russia. Aircraft from a bygone era, born in the Cold War, but still as deadly as on the first day.

The Tu-160, called "Blackjack" by NATO, had a remarkable similarity to the legendary Concorde. With an equally pointed nose and large delta wings, they were almost identical in their aerodynamic silhouette. At 54 meters in length, the Concorde was only about seven meters longer than the Russian bombers, but while one aircraft once transported businesspeople and tourists in luxury across the Atlantic, the other was created to bring death and destruction.

The bombers gleamed silver in the winter sun, their white paintwork a macabre contrast to their deadly mission. Each of the two aircraft carried four engines that devoured kerosene with a hungry roar and could bring the machines to speeds beyond the sound barrier.

Four crew members were on board each machine: pilot, co-pilot, weapons systems officer, and navigator. Men who had trained for this moment for years, hoping it would never occur. Now they sat in their air-conditioned cockpits, surrounded by blinking instruments and cutting-edge technology, and carried out orders that would forever change the history of humanity.

Those Tu-160s could approach their target at almost twice the speed of sound—faster than most interceptor fighters, faster than most air defense missiles. With an operational radius of 7000 kilometers, they could reach virtually any target in Europe from Kaliningrad, from the coasts of Portugal to the steppes of Russia, from the fjords of Norway to the Mediterranean beaches of Greece.

But it was the payload that made them the ultimate weapon of fear. With a weapons load of forty tons, those Concorde-like bombers were among the deadliest weapons in existence. As cargo, they could carry twenty-four nuclear warheads or twelve Kh-102 strategic cruise missiles with nuclear warheads. Add to that conventional bombs, anti-radar missiles, and a variety of other weapon systems, each designed to inflict massive damage.

The sky over the Baltic Sea was clear on this November day, which increased visibility but also the risk of detection. The two bombers were accompanied by thirteen Russian fighter jets—a mix of SU-35s and MiG-31s, the most modern fighters in the Russian air force arsenal. Their task was to protect the valuable bombers from enemy interceptors and clear the way for the deadly cargo.

Shortly after takeoff, the Tu-160 pilots engaged the afterburner. With an ear-shattering thunder that made the windows of houses in the wide area tremble, the bombers accelerated to twice the speed of sound. The characteristic sonic boom swept over the landscape, an acoustic omen of the impending doom.

The formation quickly climbed to its operational altitude of 12,000 meters. From here, the curvature of the Earth was clearly visible, a blue arc on the horizon that underscored the fragility of our planet. The pilots, however, had no time for such philosophical contemplations—their attention was on the instruments, the radar screens, the communication devices.

Their goal was to deliver a nuclear warning shot. To drop an atomic bomb on an air force base in Poland to force NATO to surrender, without triggering a full nuclear exchange. A dangerous game with fire, a balancing act on the edge of the abyss.

Shortly after reaching combat altitude, the two Tu-160s each fired ten of their AS-11 Killer anti-radar missiles. These highly developed weapons, designated by NATO forces as "Kh-31P" or "AS-17

Krypton," were specifically designed to locate and destroy enemy radar installations. With a range of 245 kilometers, they could be fired from a safe distance, while their solid rocket propulsion accelerated them to speeds of up to Mach 3.5—almost four times the speed of sound.

The twenty anti-radar missiles zoomed toward air defense positions and radar installations in Poland and the Baltic states, electronic bloodhounds hunting for electromagnetic prey. Their sensors actively searched for the characteristic signals of air defense radars, ready to detonate their deadly warhead once a target was acquired.

Behind them, the bombers continued, now lower and slower, to evade radar tracking. The crews sweated in their pressure suits, adrenaline making their hearts race. They knew they were making history—a history of horror.

The Tu-160s then fired a total of three of their Kh-102 cruise missiles with nuclear warheads. The launch sequence was precisely choreographed: First, the bomb bay doors opened on the underside of the aircraft, then the missiles were hydraulically positioned, finally the engines were ignited and the mechanical locks released.

The Kh-102, NATO codename "AS-15 Kent," were cruise missiles of the latest generation. With their turbojet engine, they could fly over 5,000 kilometers, hovering close to the ground to avoid radar detection, and perform complex evasive maneuvers to complicate interception attempts. Each of these cruise missiles carried a thermonuclear warhead with a yield of 350 kilotons—more than twenty times that of the Hiroshima bomb.

After the cruise missiles were fired, the bombers turned and returned to their air force base in the Kaliningrad enclave. Their mission was complete, the death sentence pronounced. The crews breathed a sigh of relief, but the tension remained. They knew that their action would trigger retaliatory measures.

Indeed, one of the Tu-160s was hit on the way back by a Polish air defense position. A Patriot missile, fired by a desperate crew who knew their last hours had struck, hit the bomber's right wing. The explosion tore off part of the wing, fuel ignited and engulfed the aircraft in a sea of flames. The pilot still tried to stabilize the severely damaged aircraft, but the aerodynamic forces were too strong. The Tu-160 spiraled toward the ground, a burning torch in the sky, before crashing in a wooded area. None of the crew members survived.

The pilots knew they had just initiated humanity's final war.

Meanwhile, all three cruise missiles with nuclear warheads reached their target in Poland. The air defense, partially blinded and deaf due to the previous attacks on their radar installations, couldn't stop them. With incredible precision, the Kh-102s navigated to their pre-programmed target points: a NATO air base near Łask, a missile defense position at Redzikowo, and a military communication center near Warsaw.

The 350-kiloton nuclear bombs exploded just above the Earth's surface to achieve maximum destructive effect. Three artificial suns glowed in the Polish sky, brighter than a thousand noon suns. The heat was so intense that people within a radius of several kilometers were instantly burned, their bodies reduced to shadows etched onto walls and streets.

The shock wave followed fractions of a second later, an invisible wall of compressed air that emanated from the explosion center at more than a thousand kilometers per hour. It shattered buildings, uprooted trees, transformed cars and trucks into deadly projectiles. People were tossed through the air like toy figures, their bodies crushed by the unimaginable force.

Then the characteristic mushroom clouds rose, these eerie emblems of the atomic age. They grew into the sky, first straight, then widened into the familiar mushroom shape. Dust particles, debris, and radioactive material were hurled into the atmosphere, where they were caught by the winds and would be distributed over hundreds, sometimes thousands of kilometers—the infamous fallout that would continue to kill long after the actual explosion.

The news of the nuclear detonations in Poland spread around the world at the speed of light. In Washington, London, Paris, Berlin—everywhere crisis teams were convened, emergency plans activated, civil protection measures initiated. But it was already too late for diplomacy, too late for negotiations, too late for reason.

NATO, prepared for such a moment since its founding and yet hopelessly unprepared for its actual reality, responded with the only language that was still understood in this situation: violence.

After the Russian nuclear weapons had detonated, NATO launched a small bomber fleet from Ramstein Air Base in Germany, the headquarters of the US Air Force in Europe. Ramstein, with its 4.5-kilometer-long runway, extensive hangars, and maintenance facilities, was the heart of US air power in Europe. From here, operations could be coordinated and conducted throughout Europe, the Middle East, and parts of Africa.

The bomber fleet consisted of four B-1B Lancers, strategic long-range bombers of the US Air Force. These impressive machines, over 44 meters long with a wingspan of more than 41 meters in extended position, were true masterpieces of aviation engineering. With their variable geometry wings, they could operate optimally both in high-speed flight and during slow approach to the target.

Those B-1Bs had been in service since about the mid-nineties, constantly modernized and improved to keep pace with evolving threats. With an operational radius of about 5000 kilometers and a maximum speed of about 1.2 times the speed of sound, they were among the most modern and powerful American bombers, surpassed only by the newer B-2 Spirit with its stealth technology.

The four bombers, accompanied by F-22 Raptor fighter jets for air protection and EA-18G Growlers for electronic warfare, took off in perfect formation. Their mission was clear: retaliation for the nuclear attack on Poland, a NATO member. Their target was the Kaliningrad enclave, the heart of the Russian military presence on the Baltic Sea and starting point of the attack.

The flight from Ramstein to Kaliningrad took about two hours. The bomber crews, highly trained professionals in their air-conditioned cockpits, felt the gravity of their task. Most of them were younger than the aircraft they were flying, born after the end of the Cold War, raised in a world where nuclear conflict was considered a distant theoretical risk. Now they were the executors of a judgment that could possibly mean the end of human civilization.

As they approached Kaliningrad, they were acquired by Russian air defense systems. The notorious S-400 Triumf system, one of the most advanced air defense systems in the world, could detect targets at distances of up to 400 kilometers and engage them at up to 250 kilometers. The B-1B crews knew they had been detected, but their electronic countermeasures and the escort of the EA-18G Growlers should give them an advantage.

The S-400 missiles were fired, white contrails marking their deadly flight paths in the blue sky. The F-22 Raptors reacted immediately, firing their own air-to-ground missiles to neutralize the threat, while the Growlers opened intense electronic jamming to confuse the S-400's targeting systems.

A desperate air battle erupted as the B-1Bs approached their targets. Russian fighter planes—mainly SU-35s and MiG-31s—rose to intercept the intruders. The skies over the Baltic Sea became the scene of a futuristic gladiatorial fight as jets at multiple times the speed of sound danced around each other, fired missiles, and performed desperate evasive maneuvers.

Despite the fierce resistance, all four B-1Bs reached their target, 600 kilometers in front of Kaliningrad they opened their bomb bays and released their deadly cargo: cruise missiles equipped with tactical nuclear weapons, each with a yield of about 300 kilotons.

The detonations followed a few minutes later. Four nuclear flashes illuminated Kaliningrad, the former Königsberg, a city with a rich history that now went up in nuclear fire. The historic old town, the cathedral, the university where Immanuel Kant once taught—everything was obliterated in fractions of a second, reduced to radioactive ash.

The city was destroyed, its 450,000 inhabitants wiped out in an instant. What was once a thriving metropolis, a center of culture and commerce, became a nuclear graveyard, a radioactive wasteland that would be uninhabitable for generations.

The B-1Bs turned away, their mission accomplished.

Thus began the nuclear exchange that would change the world forever. One attack led to a counterattack, one escalation to the next. The spiral of violence, once set in motion, could no longer be stopped.

CHAPTER 6: THE EXCHANGE BEGINS

On the radio, the Thompsons heard the news they had feared most. The news announcer's voice trembled slightly as he said: "The Russian city of Kaliningrad has just been hit by a nuclear weapon."

The words hung in the air-conditioned interior of the Land Rover like toxic spores. David cursed softly, a single word that summarized all his despair and anger. His hands gripped the steering wheel so tightly that his knuckles stood out white, as if they wanted to break through the skin. The leather covers of the steering wheel creaked under his increased grip.

Eva placed her hand on his arm, a silent gesture of comfort and solidarity. Her fingers trembled slightly, but she tried to be strong for him, as she had always been in times of crisis. In the rearview mirror, she could see the pale faces of her children—Tim, who sat with big, questioning eyes, still too young to comprehend the full extent of the situation, and Emma, who was crying silent tears, her face a mirror of the horror they all felt.

The traffic on the highways was still moving, albeit haltingly. On the M3, which they were currently traveling on, traffic jams formed repeatedly as vehicles broke down or drivers lost control in panic. Several times they had to swerve onto the hard shoulder to avoid accidents. Sometimes it stalled, but by and large, they were still making good progress.

Particularly noticeable was that the lane into London was almost empty. No commuters, no delivery vans, no tourists—nobody wanted to go into the city. Everyone wanted out, a mass exodus reminiscent of biblical scenes. The traffic on the other side of the central barriers was an uninterrupted stream of vehicles of all kinds: limousines, SUVs, motorhomes, motorcycles, even some bicycles, whose riders desperately tried to keep pace with the motorized traffic.

David navigated through this chaos with the concentration of a surgeon during a complicated operation. His eyes constantly flitted between the road ahead, the side mirrors, and the rearview mirror, always looking for potential dangers or shortcuts.

"I think we should get off the highway," he finally said to Eva, while slowing down to avoid a wildly swerving motorcycle. "The next exit leads towards Winchester. From there, we can take country roads. They might not be as fast, but safer and probably less congested."

Eva nodded silently. She trusted his judgment in these matters. David had always had a strong sense of direction and knew the roads of southern England like the back of his hand, thanks to his numerous business trips and the weekend excursions they had taken so often, in another time, in another world.

Meanwhile in Europe, Russia launched bomber fleets and short-range missiles. The command centers deep beneath the Kremlin and in the Defense Ministry in Moscow were on highest alert. Officers in immaculately ironed uniforms, with expressionless faces and mechanical movements, carried out the orders they had practiced for years in simulations.

The approximately three hundred nuclear warheads, targeted against NATO bases and selected cities, including London, Paris, Berlin, and Rome, were already on their way. An arsenal of death, hovering over Europe like the Grim Reaper's scythe, ready to extinguish a civilization that had taken millennia to develop.

The weapons systems were diverse and sophisticated: Iskander missiles fired from mobile launch platforms at the borders to NATO countries; Kalibr cruise missiles launched from submarines in the Baltic Sea and the North Sea; strategic bombers of the Tu-95 and Tu-160 type taking off from bases deep in the Russian hinterland; and of course the feared SS-18 "Satan" and the newer RS-28 "Sarmat" intercontinental missiles, rising from their silos in the Russian steppe like apocalyptic ghosts.

Each of these weapons carried at least one nuclear warhead, many carried several, thanks to MIRV (Multiple Independently targetable Reentry Vehicle) technology, which allowed a single missile to attack up to 15 separate targets. The yield varied from "tactical" 5-kiloton weapons to strategic monsters with 800 kilotons or more—each a multiple of the bombs that had destroyed Hiroshima and Nagasaki.

When NATO learned of this massive attack, it in turn launched more bomber fleets and activated its own nuclear forces. The American Ohio-class submarines, each equipped with 24 Trident II missiles, surfaced from their hiding places in the depths of the world's oceans to deliver their deadly cargo. B-52 bombers, those flying dinosaurs of the Cold War that had been in service since the 1950s, took off from bases in Great Britain, Germany, and Italy, loaded with cruise missiles and free-fall bombs.

About 170 nuclear warheads were to hit targets in western Russia—military bases, command centers, communication nodes, transport infrastructure, and some cities of strategic importance. The logic of nuclear war was cold and inhuman: One did not target the population per se, but the enemy's ability to wage war. That millions of civilians would die in the process was "collateral damage," a term that only poorly veiled the inhumanity of the whole enterprise.

The death toll in Europe mounted at a pace that defied imagination. In the first hours of this Armageddon, as nuclear weapons detonated over major cities, military bases, and industrial centers, the number of those immediately killed rose to about 3.5 million. People who were burned by the heat flashes, who were shattered by the pressure wave, who were buried under collapsing buildings, or who simply vaporized if they were close enough to the explosion center.

This number did not account for the wounded who would die from their injuries in the coming days, without medical care in a world where hospitals were destroyed and doctors dead or fleeing. It did not account for the millions who would die in the following weeks and months from radiation sickness, hunger, or from the collapsing infrastructure. And it did not account for the long-term consequences: cancer, genetic damage, infertility, and the psychological traumas that would shape generations.

The Thompsons had left the highway and were now driving on a two-lane country road through the gentle hills of Hampshire. The landscape was idyllic, with lush green pastures where sheep grazed, old stone walls that bordered the fields, and occasional villages with their characteristic church towers and pubs.

It was a scene that had hardly changed for centuries, a postcard of rural England. But today a shadow lay over this idyll. The villages they drove through showed signs of unusual activity: people loading cars, discussing in groups in the village squares, or barricading their houses. In one place, they saw a long line in front of the local grocery store, while the village policeman vainly tried to maintain order.

"Daddy, I'm hungry," Tim said quietly from the back seat. His small voice tore David from his gloomy thoughts.

"We have sandwiches in the cooler," Eva answered, before David could react. She turned around and handed her son a sandwich wrapped in aluminum foil. "It's ham and cheese, your favorite sandwich."

Tim gratefully accepted it, his little face brightening briefly. "Thank you, Mummy."

Eva also handed Emma a sandwich, which she held only listlessly in her hands. "You should eat something, darling," Eva urged. "We all need our strength."

Emma nodded mechanically and slowly began to unwrap the foil. Her appetite had vanished, stifled by the fear and shock, but she knew her mother was right. They had to remain functional.

David also accepted a sandwich when Eva handed him one and bit into it, without really tasting what he was eating. His thoughts raced, plans formed and dissolved again in his head, as he tried to calculate their chances of survival in various scenarios.

The Land Rover drove on, its robust tires rolling over the asphalt, while the diesel engine steadily hummed—a reassuring, constant sound in a world that had come apart at the seams. They passed fields and forests, crossed small rivers, and drove through villages whose names were barely readable on the weathered signs.

The sun stood high in the sky, a radiantly blue November day, inappropriately peaceful for the apocalyptic events that were unfolding. The radio continued to provide fragmentary information, interrupted by static noise and occasional outages when they drove through valleys or dense forests that disturbed the signal.

They learned of more nuclear explosions throughout Europe: Brussels, the heart of the EU, had been hit; Frankfurt, Germany's financial center; Marseille, France's most important port. The bombing targets seemed to be a mix of military logic and political symbolism, a final, desperate attempt to break the enemy not only physically but also morally.

The NATO response was equally devastating: St. Petersburg, the former capital of the

Tsarist Empire, lay in ruins; Murmansk, Russia's most important arctic port, was obliterated; Kaliningrad, as they already knew, practically no longer existed.

It was as if an invisible hand was wiping across a map of Europe and erasing cities that had existed for centuries, sometimes millennia. Cities that had survived wars, pestilence, revolutions, and natural disasters were now extinguished in fractions of a second, reduced to radioactive craters and irradiated ruins.

"Will it hit us too?" Emma suddenly asked, her voice barely more than a whisper.

David and Eva exchanged a glance, a silent conversation between spouses who knew each other well enough to communicate without words.

"We are on our way to Uncle Ben," David finally answered, carefully choosing his words. "His house is far away from large cities or military installations. We should be safe there."

It was a half-truth. No one could guarantee safety in this new reality. The fallout would spread over hundreds of kilometers, carried by winds and rainfall. The electromagnetic pulses from the explosions could destroy electronic devices over a wide area. And then there were the long-term consequences: the nuclear winter, the collapsing trade, the return to more primitive forms of life in a world without reliable energy, modern medicine, or industrial agriculture.

But the children didn't need to know that now. Now they needed hope, a plan, a goal. The cruel truths of the post-nuclear war world would reach them soon enough.

They drove on, as the day progressed and the sun slowly moved westward. Traffic on the country roads increased, as more and more people left the main arteries to escape the congestion and panic. David had to swerve several times onto unpaved side roads to make progress, sometimes even across field paths where the Land Rover could play out its superior off-road capability.

The fuel gauge showed about half a tank, enough to reach Ben's house if no unforeseen detours became necessary. The additional canisters in the trunk gave them a certain security, but David knew that fuel would become the most precious commodity in the coming days and weeks, more valuable than gold or diamonds.

As they reached a rise, David briefly stopped to let his gaze sweep over the landscape. In the distance, far to the east, they could see a strange, reddish shimmer on the horizon, like an unnatural sunset on the wrong side of the sky.

"What is that?" asked Eva, as she followed his gaze.

David didn't answer immediately. He knew what it was, but the words stuck in his throat. Finally, with a rough voice, he said: "London. It's burning."

They stared silently at the distant glow, unable to avert their gaze from this evidence of the demise of their world. The city where they had lived, where their children had been born, where they had laughed and cried and loved, was now just a fireball on the horizon, a monument to human madness.

A soft sob tore them from their trance. Tim was crying, his small body shaking with suppressed tears. Emma put an arm around her brother and pulled him close, her own tears flowing unhindered down her cheeks.

"Come, let's drive on," David said softly and started the engine again. "We need to be at Ben's before nightfall."

They continued their journey, while behind them the ashes of what had once been their home rose into the sky, carried by columns of smoke that pointed like accusing fingers at the gods.

But they were lucky, a Pegasus rocket had been able to destroy the Russian EMP satellite that was supposed to explode between the two nuclear powers England and France. Thus, there was no large-scale EMP.

CHAPTER 7: THE TRAFFIC JAM

The Thompsons had now left London far behind. The Land Rover wound its way through the curvy country roads of southern England, past gentle, green hills and occasional villages with their characteristic stone houses and ancient church towers. A mist-shrouded ray of sunlight fought its way through the gray cloud cover and made the autumnal landscape appear in a strangely unreal light—as if a painter from another time had captured this moment with melancholic brush strokes on a canvas.

David had chosen a side route that led them on narrow roads towards the southwest, away from the overcrowded main arteries. This decision had initially proven wise. The small village roads were not designed for speed, but they were relatively empty, apart from the occasional tractors or local vehicles. The robust suspension of the Land Rover swallowed the unevenness of the old asphalt surface, while the diesel engine with its deep hum provided a reassuring background noise—an anchor of normality in a world that had come apart at the seams.

After about an hour on these winding paths, however, they had to turn onto a larger connecting road that linked several coastal towns. And here their progress began to stall. What at first looked like normal traffic soon condensed into a thick, barely moving mass of vehicles of all kinds.

The traffic began to stall. Cars lined up bumper to bumper, like a metal snake that wound sluggishly through the landscape. The drivers honked impatiently, although it obviously didn't help. Some got out to peer ahead, in the vain hope of being able to identify the cause of the jam. The air was filled with the smell of overheated engines and the barely perceptible but nevertheless disturbing hint of panic.

The longer they stood in the traffic jam, the more nervous David became. His fingers drummed an irregular rhythm on the steering wheel, while his eyes constantly wandered between the road ahead of them and the rearview mirror. Eva placed a reassuring hand on his arm, but her face also reflected the growing concern.

"What do you think, how long will we be stuck here?" she asked quietly, trying to keep her voice calm so that the children in the back seat couldn't hear her.

David shook his head. "No idea. But we need to find

a way to get out of here. We can't just stand in traffic and wait."

With every inch they moved forward, the frustration grew. The minutes stretched into hours, as the sun slowly sank lower and cast long shadows over the landscape. Tim had fallen asleep in the back seat, his head lying heavily on Emma's shoulder. She absentmindedly stroked his hair, while her gaze thoughtfully wandered out the window, to the passing fields and forests that looked so peaceful, so untouched by the chaos that had gripped the world.

After what felt like an eternity, they could finally see the cause of the traffic jam. A car had broken down in the middle of the road, the driver had gotten out. It was an old, rusty Ford Fiesta, whose engine had obviously given up the ghost. The hood was open, and a small cloud of smoke rose from it—a clear sign of an overheated or completely defective engine.

The driver, a thin middle-aged man in a worn suit, stood next to the vehicle and gestured wildly. His glasses sat crookedly on his nose, and his face was reddened from excitement or exertion. He was desperately trying to get the attention of passing drivers, probably hoping for help.

As the man tried to run across the hard shoulder to stop a passing truck, the accident happened. The vehicles that were passing the broken-down car had accelerated, relieved to finally leave the obstacle behind. The man seemed to have misjudged the speed. He stepped onto the roadway, directly into the path of an approaching small truck.

There was a dull impact, a brief, startled honking, and then the figure of the man was hurled through the air like a puppet whose strings had been cut. He landed hard on the asphalt, rolled several meters further, and then lay motionless.

The small truck stopped briefly, but instead of getting out and helping, the driver, after a short moment of hesitation, gave gas again and drove away—a hit-and-run that would have been unthinkable in normal times, but seemed all too understandable in this new reality of chaos and fear.

The corpse of the man now lay on the hard shoulder, a grotesque obstacle that exacerbated the already tense situation. Blood seeped onto the gray asphalt, forming a dark pool that slowly spread.

Cars and trucks swerved and drove along the hard shoulder to escape the traffic jam that had formed behind the broken-down vehicle. They simply drove over the corpse, as if it were nothing more than another obstacle in their desperate flight. The dull sound when tires rolled over flesh and bone was audible even with closed windows—a wet, cracking sound that echoed in the gut.

As the Thompsons approached, David saw that a corpse lay on the hard shoulder. The vehicles drove more slowly there, but it was moving forward. The image was surreal and frightening at the same time: a human body, already deformed by the vehicles driving over it, lay stretched out on the dirty asphalt like a grotesque sculpture.

"David, what's up ahead?" said Eva, whose horror was clearly visible in her face. She had leaned slightly forward to see better, but as she took in the scene, she recoiled, a hand over her mouth.

"There's a corpse lying there," David said with a rough voice. He swallowed hard, his Adam's apple visibly moving under the tense skin of his throat.

"But you're not going to drive over it too, are you?" Eva said almost panicking, her eyes wide with horror. The mere thought made her stomach turn.

David looked left and right, desperately searching for an alternative. "Yes. We can't get onto the other lane. They won't let us merge," he finally said resignedly. The traffic on the main lane was moving slowly but steadily. The drivers there were not willing to let someone from the hard shoulder cut in—a selfish but human reaction in a situation of general panic.

They were directly behind a dark blue station wagon that turned onto the hard shoulder. David followed it and also drove onto the hard shoulder. "The sooner, the better," he thought. If they merged now, maybe they wouldn't have to drive directly over the body, but could drive around it or at least only graze its edge.

"Oh God. The children," said Eva and turned to the children. Her face was chalk-white, the freckles on her nose standing out clearly like dark dots on white paper. "Close your eyes," Eva said panically to her children, who were sitting in the back seat and looking out the windows, still unaware of what they would soon see.

"Did you hear? Close your eyes for as long as I tell you to," she said again very emphatically to them, her voice trembling with suppressed panic.

Emma and Tim nodded and closed their eyes. Tim's small fingers clung to the plush dinosaur he carried with him, while Emma folded her hands firmly in her lap, the knuckles white with tension.

Just before the corpse, the cars slowed down and then drove slowly over it. The station wagon in front of them drove slowly over the corpse. The car lifted slightly, an eerie rocking, as if it were driving over an uneven threshold. Eva was startled and gasped loudly, her body tensing like a bowstring, ready to protect the children, although the danger was not physical but psychological—the sight of human mortality in its rawest form.

David almost had to vomit as well. The corpse had been totally crushed by the many vehicles that had already driven over it. There was blood everywhere. Intestines spilled out from the stomach area, shimmering and wet in the sunlight. Bluish-gray intestinal loops lay on the road like bizarre snakes. On the torso, one could see the traces of the tires, deep furrows in the flesh where the rubber had dug into the soft tissues. The ribcage was caved in, ribs protruding like broken spears from the torn flesh. The man's face was unrecognizable, just a bloody mush in which a single eye was still recognizable, wide open in eternal horror.

"David," Eva screamed as they were about to drive over it. She screamed in panic with horror, unable to avert her gaze, although every fiber of her being screamed to close her eyes and block out the cruel reality.

David's stomach turned as well. He had to suppress the urge to gag when he saw the corpse. A sour taste rose in his throat, and cold sweat broke out on his forehead. He tried to suppress his emotions and concentrated on driving over it. With utmost concentration, he steered the Land Rover, trying to avoid the most sensitive parts of the destroyed body.

Slowly he drove over it. He tried as much as possible not to drive over the torso, but the body parts were scattered around, it was impossible to avoid them all. When one of the rear tires lifted slightly, he just thought: "Shit. Such shit." The thought that there might now be body parts on the rear wheel almost made David's blood freeze in his veins. A terrible thought that made him shudder, as if an icy hand were stroking over his back.

Slowly he drove on and then accelerated to get away from this place of horror as quickly as possible. "You can open your eyes again," David said, trying to appear normal and not show anything. However, his voice sounded tense and brittle, like a thin piece of glass that could break at any moment.

Eva was still quietly sobbing, her body shaking with sobs that she tried to suppress. She wiped her eyes with the sleeve of her blouse, leaving mascara streaks on the light fabric.

Emma and Tim cautiously opened their eyes, unsure what they would see. Tim looked questioningly at his sister, who just shook her head and squeezed his hand—a silent request not to ask, not to know.

David drove on, while the image of the crushed corpse burned into his memory like a glowing iron. He knew he would never forget it, that it would haunt him in his dreams, a cruel memorial to the fragility of human life and the brutality of a world in chaos.

The traffic gradually dissolved as they left the accident scene behind. The road became wider, and the vehicles spread out, each searching for the fastest way to supposed safety. There were no more rules, no courtesy, only the naked survival instinct.

In the distance, they could already see the gentle hills that led to Ben's house. Just a few more hours, and they would be there, in relative safety. David pressed the gas pedal all the way down, the engine howled, and the Land Rover accelerated, as if it too wanted to escape death.

CHAPTER 8: THE CITIES DISAPPEAR

The Thompsons were now driving along a winding country road that snaked through the gentle hills of Cornwall. The Land Rover effortlessly climbed the steep inclines and glided down the slopes, its robust diesel engine humming steadily like a patient workhorse. The road was lined with ancient stone walls, overgrown with moss and lichens—silent witnesses to a centuries-old cultural landscape that now stood on the brink of extinction.

The autumn sky above them was of a strange, unreal clarity. No airplane drew its white contrails through the blue, no birds circled in the air. It was as if nature itself had held its breath, in anticipation of the coming apocalypse.

David had avoided the larger towns as best he could. He knew this area well, had often vacationed in Cornwall in his youth, and later explored the hidden bays and picturesque villages with Eva and the children. This familiarity now proved life-saving. He chose remote side roads and seldom-traveled paths that weren't marked on any tourist map, to escape the masses of fleeing people and make faster progress.

He knew that the larger cities would most likely be targets. Plymouth, Exeter, Bristol—all places of strategic importance, whether through ports, military installations, or industrial facilities. Places that would be marked on Russian target maps if it came to the worst.

"How far is it to Uncle Ben's?" asked Tim from the back seat, his voice quiet and tired after the rigors of the long journey. His eyes were red from crying, but he had bravely maintained his composure, more than could be expected from a seven-year-old.

"Not far now, darling," Eva answered, although she didn't know exactly herself. She half turned and gently stroked her son's tousled blond hair. "Maybe another hour."

"More like an hour and a half," David quietly corrected, trying to remain realistic. "But we're making good progress."

Emma, who had been silently staring out the window, suddenly jumped and pressed her face against the glass. "Dad! Look!" she called with a choked voice and pointed eastward.

David slowed the car and followed her gaze. What

he saw made his blood freeze.

In the far distance, on the eastern horizon, they saw as in a ghost vision how London was hit by several nuclear weapons. Due to the good weather, one could see multiple mushroom clouds growing into the sky above the city—gigantic, deadly flowers of fire and destruction, stretching their stems from the dying heart of the metropolis.

The sight was of a cruel beauty, an apocalyptic mirage announcing the end of a civilization. The mushroom clouds rose majestically, their upper edges glowing golden in the sunlight, while their bases shimmered in gloomy, toxic grays and blacks.

Even further in the distance, they could make out more mushroom clouds, which over destroyed English cities suggested a picture of horror. Manchester, Birmingham, Glasgow, Belfast—all major urban centers of the United Kingdom became victims of the nuclear inferno.

Eva let out a suppressed cry and clapped her hand over her mouth. The cruel reality of what was happening hit her with full force. Millions of people who lived in these cities had been extinguished in a moment—families, children, old people, all gone in a flash of light and heat that was more intense than a thousand suns.

"My God," she whispered, tears running unhindered down her cheeks. "All those people..."

David couldn't say anything. His throat was constricted, a heavy lump of unspoken grief and horror blocked every word. He steered the car to the roadside and stopped, unable to drive on in the face of this sight of the end of the world.

They weren't the only ones who had stopped. On the narrow strip of land that offered a panoramic view over the landscape, several vehicles had stopped. The drivers and passengers had gotten out and stood in small groups, some crying, some praying, all united in their horror.

An old man in a crumpled gray suit leaned against his antiquated Morris Minor, his face buried in his hands. A young mother held her baby tightly against her, as if she could protect it from the cruel reality. A teenager in a school uniform stared emptily into the distance, his features frozen in an expression of incredulous horror.

First there was a bright flash, so bright that it outshone the sun, a supernatural light that for a brief moment transformed the entire landscape into a ghostly relief. Then they saw how the behemoth grew into the sky—a boiling, writhing column of fire and smoke that screwed higher and higher until it reached the stratosphere. The fireball, the core of the explosion, grew upward and simultaneously began to expand, an extending inferno that devoured everything that came within its radius.

After a few minutes, the mushroom clouds

had reached their maximum height and grew only sideways, forming the characteristic shape that had become the symbol of nuclear annihilation since Hiroshima and Nagasaki. Smaller condensation clouds formed around the edges, like dirty cotton balls clinging to the main body of the cloud.

"Fortunately, we're far enough away," David said quietly, more to himself than to his family. There was no danger at that distance that they could be blinded by the initial light flash of the detonation. But still, he had drummed into his children not to look at the explosions. But it was terrible, just the thought of how many people were dead there now. In his mind, he saw the images he knew from documentaries about Hiroshima—burned bodies, shadows of people that were etched onto walls, buildings that collapsed like houses of cards under the unimaginable force of the pressure wave.

The motorists who had stopped stood silently, united in a moment of collective mourning. Then the silence broke as one of them pointed to the sky. "Look!"

At a great height, where the air was thin and clear, they saw Russian bombers and fighter planes. The massive Tu-95 "Bear" bombers with their characteristic contra-rotating propellers were clearly recognizable, accompanied by the slim, dangerous silhouettes of the Su-57 stealth fighters. They were engaged in combat with

English fighter planes—Typhoons and F-35s, which tried to intercept the intruders in desperate, artful maneuvers.

It was a surreal spectacle, like from a science fiction film, but the stakes were higher than in any fiction. The silver dots in the sky, circling each other in a deadly dance, decided the fate of millions.

One of the bombers, a Tupolev Tu-95 with four piston engines that produced an ear-deafening noise, was hit by a British Typhoon fighter. An air-to-air missile hit the bomber's right wing, and for a moment nothing seemed to happen. Then the fuel tank exploded in an orange-red fireball. The massive machine broke apart, debris and burning fuel rained from the sky like a deadly hail.

The other bombers caught fire. Hit, they drew a dark plume of smoke behind them, black streaks that stretched across the blue sky like ominous signs. They rapidly lost altitude, their wings broke, their fuselages burst, as they tumbled toward the inevitable fall into the depths.

Some of the spectators at the roadside began to cheer, a brief, almost hysterical outburst of triumph amid the horror. "Yes, show those Russians! Give it to them!" shouted a man with a red face and clenched fists, as if he were at a football game and not at the end of the world.

David silently observed how one of the bombers

went into a spin. The massive machine rotated uncontrollably around its longitudinal axis, while one of the wings tore off, separated from the fuselage by the centrifugal forces acting on the damaged structure. The bomber plunged steeply downward, a burning meteor returning to earth.

Another bomber came ever closer to them, its course unpredictable, its fate sealed. It was rapidly losing altitude, the smoke from its destroyed engines drawing a black line in the sky, like an ominous prophecy.

"Oh, damn, that thing is going to crash near here," said one of the spectators, his voice breaking with panic. The realization that the burning colossus was plunging directly toward them hit everyone simultaneously.

"Run!" someone shouted, and suddenly the paralysis dissolved. People ran in all directions, stumbled over uneven ground, pushed each other aside, driven by the oldest of all instincts—the will to survive.

David grabbed Eva by the arm. "To the car! Quick!"

But Eva shook her head. "No time! We have to get away from the road!" She grabbed Tim, while David took Emma by the arm. Together they ran across the road to the other field, following the others in their flight from the approaching death from the sky.

The Thompson family ran as fast as their legs

could carry them. Tim stumbled, and David lifted him with one arm, carried him like a sack, while with the other hand he pulled Emma close to him. Eva ran beside them, her face contorted with exertion and fear.

About three hundred fifty meters from the road, the bomber bored into a brown field that had recently been plowed and now waited like a fresh grave for its metal inhabitant. The earth trembled under the impact, the sound was deafening—a deep booming crash, followed by the shrill screeching of bending metal.

Like an accordion, the fuselage was folded together, crushed under the unimaginable force of the impact. The wings broke off, the engines tore from their mountings, while the massive fuselage penetrated ever deeper into the soft ground, leaving a swath of destruction behind it.

There was a loud explosion as the remains of the fuel and the ammunition on board detonated. A pillar of fire shot into the sky, followed by a pressure wave that pulsed through the air and threw the fleeing people to the ground. Wreckage flew around, deadly projectiles of bent metal and broken composite materials that whizzed through the air and came down all around them.

Some were still running, driven by panic fear, but some stopped and looked around, the worst apparently over. A fire was blazing near the wreck, blazing with hungry flames that reached for everything that was flammable. Residual fuel burned with a deep black plume of smoke that laid itself like an ominous veil over the landscape.

The Thompsons stood on the field, earth and grass sticking to their clothes, small cuts and abrasions testifying to their hasty retreat. They stared at the wreck, hypnotized by the destruction, unable to avert their gaze from this bizarre artwork of war.

"I hope they were on their way back and no longer had atomic bombs on board," said a man beside them anxiously, his voice barely more than a whisper. He was about David's age, wore a tattered tweed jacket and rimless glasses that sat crookedly on his nose. His face was pale, his eyes wide behind the glasses.

"Such bombs can withstand a lot. Even in peacetime, there were crashes with nuclear weapons," David answered seriously. He thought of the Palomares incident in Spain in 1966, when an American B-52 bomber with four hydrogen bombs on board crashed. Three of the bombs were found on land, a fourth fell into the Mediterranean and was only recovered after a two-month search and recovery operation. None of the warheads detonated at that time, but it was a disturbing example of how close the world had already stood to the abyss several times.

The spectators began to move slowly, first hesitantly, then with growing determination. They returned to their vehicles, trying to find normality in a situation that was beyond all norms.

Slowly, the Thompsons also went back to the road, where their Land Rover stood. Small wreckage pieces were scattered on the road—bent metal pieces, fragments of the instrument panel, a tattered piece of fabric that might once have been the uniform of a Russian pilot. Silent witnesses to a tragedy that was playing out in manifold versions across the skies of Great Britain.

They got back into the car, silently, each absorbed in their own gloomy thoughts. David started the engine, whose familiar hum sounded strangely reassuring in this world that was breaking into pieces. He put the car in gear and drove off slowly, carefully maneuvering around the debris scattered on the road.

As they left the crash site behind, Eva turned her gaze back. The burning wreck was like a macabre monument, a tomb for the crew who had presumably been killed instantly, but also a symbol for the greater tragedy that was unfolding around them. She wondered if the men in this plane had known what they were doing, if they had thought of their families, of their children, of their future, which they destroyed a bit more with each warhead dropped.

The journey continued, through a landscape that paradoxically seemed more peaceful than ever before. The fields and forests, the rivers and hills

—they all continued to exist, unimpressed by the human dramas playing out on their surface. A flock of sheep grazed peacefully on a meadow, a fox darted across a field path, birds twittered in the trees. Nature followed its own rhythm, unconcerned about humanity's self-destruction.

In a way, it was comforting, David thought, as he steered the car along the winding country road. No matter what humanity did, the earth would continue. Perhaps not with us, but it would recover, as it had after many catastrophes. Life would return, in new forms, with new adaptations. The great cycles of the planet would continue, long after the last human had disappeared.

These thoughts offered a strange comfort as they drove toward their uncertain future.

CHAPTER 9: THE BEGINNING OF THE END OF THE WORLD

Many European cities and NATO bases were destroyed during the Russian attack. The map of the once proud continent transformed into a patchwork of radioactive craters and smoking ruins. Paris, Berlin, Rome, Madrid, Brussels—the capitals of Europe, centers of culture and history, cradles of Western civilization, were transformed into irradiated wastelands within minutes.

The historical landmarks that had survived for centuries no longer existed. The Eiffel Tower, the Brandenburg Gate, the Colosseum, Buckingham Palace—all these symbols of human creativity and endurance had crumbled to dust. Where once the gothic spires of Cologne Cathedral reached into the sky, there now gaped a crater several hundred meters in diameter. The dome of St. Peter's Basilica, Michelangelo's masterpiece, had collapsed, burying beneath it the priceless artworks of generations.

But the physical destruction was only the beginning. The true extent of the catastrophe was revealed in the human losses. In Paris alone, over two million people died—vaporized by the heat, torn apart by the pressure wave, or buried under the ruins of their once proud city-state. In Berlin, it was 1.7 million, in Rome 1.2 million, in London, as the Thompsons had seen with their own eyes, nearly three million.

The survivors in the outskirts of the cities soon envied the dead. With severe burns, radiation-induced illness, and without medical care, they were doomed to die—a slow, agonizing death that could drag on for days or weeks.

As American bombers crossed the border into Russia, Russia launched several hundred short-range missiles and ICBMs from northern Russia near Scandinavia and southwestern Russia near Ukraine. The silos opened like mechanical blossoms, and the missiles rose, carried by their fire tails that turned night into day.

The missile stations in the taiga, hidden under camouflage nets and false forest landscapes, were activated. Commanders, who had trained for this moment for years, turned their keys and entered their codes, each movement precise and methodical, as practiced in hundreds of drills. The chain of command functioned, the systems responded, the protocols were followed—a deadly symphony of efficiency.

The SS-18 Satan, some of the most powerful nuclear weapons of all time, left their underground dwellings. Each of these missiles carried up to ten independently targetable nuclear warheads, each with a yield of up to 750 kilotons—fifty times stronger than the bomb that destroyed Hiroshima. The newer RS-28 Sarmat, called "Satan II" by NATO, were even more threatening: up to 15 warheads per missile, each with a yield of over a megaton.

The USA in turn launched about six hundred nuclear warheads from missile silos, most of them located in the heart and north of the USA, and from nuclear submarines in the Atlantic and Pacific against Russia. The American Minuteman III ICBMs rose from their underground silos in North Dakota, Wyoming, and Montana, while the Trident II missiles were fired from the depths of the oceans, where the Ohio-class submarines had kept their deadly cargo ready.

An American satellite, which according to agreements shouldn't have existed, launched a salvo of seven nuclear warheads meant to destroy Russian missile silos in Siberia. This satellite, part of the strictly secret "Mjolnir" program, had been launched into space under the guise of a weather observation station. Its true nature as an orbital nuclear platform had violated several international treaties, but in the heat of the nuclear exchange, such treaty breaches no longer mattered.

With the launch of the ICBMs, the Russians also launched ICBMs from missile bases and nuclear submarines against the USA and Canada. The Russian submarines of the Borei class, lurking in the depths of the Arctic Ocean and the North Pacific, fired their Bulava missiles. These underwater giants, almost invisible to NATO's detection systems, had waited for weeks in silent readiness, buried in the mud of the seabed or hidden under the Arctic ice cap.

Missiles struck all over the USA. The sky over the American continent was illuminated by the fireballs of nuclear detonations—an apocalyptic firework that marked the end of an era. The strategic targets were hit with merciless precision: military bases, command centers, communication nodes, transportation hubs.

All airports and all major cities were destroyed. New York, Chicago, Los Angeles, Houston, Philadelphia—America's vibrant metropolises transformed into piles of ash. The iconic skylines that had graced postcards and films for decades no longer existed. The Empire State Building, the Golden Gate Bridge, the Willis Tower, the

Hollywood sign—all these symbols of American greatness and engineering were obliterated.

All naval bases and army bases were reduced to rubble. Pearl Harbor, Norfolk, San Diego, Fort Bragg, Fort Hood—the most powerful military installations in the world, once impregnable fortresses of American power, were now radioactive craters. The proud fleets of the US Navy, carrier groups and destroyer squadrons, were caught at the pier and annihilated, their sophisticated defense systems powerless against the overwhelming number of incoming warheads.

Several Russian nuclear weapons also struck the Panama Canal, to destroy this crucial canal forever. The narrow waterway that connected the Atlantic with the Pacific and had been a cornerstone of global trade since its opening in 1914 was made impassable by a series of strategically placed detonations. The massive lock gates, masterpieces of engineering, were torn from their anchors, the canal beds filled with debris and radioactive rubble. A century of human effort was undone in seconds.

The Russians had about 1.7 times more nuclear weapons available than the Americans, partly because they weren't so strict about the disarmament agreements they had once made. While the United States had at least superficially tried to adhere to the provisions of the New START treaty, Russia had secretly continued to arm. Underground repositories in the vastness of Siberia, hidden under decoy buildings or natural landscape features, housed hundreds of undeclared warheads.

The largest nuclear weapon, a modified version of the legendary "Tsar" bomb, which at fifty-seven megatons was about three times stronger than the strongest American nuclear weapon, hit New York. The original Tsar bomb, which had been detonated for test purposes over Novaya Zemlya in 1961, had already overshadowed all previous nuclear weapons with its 50 megatons. This new version, developed in secret and kept as a final insurance, even surpassed this record.

Another of these monstrous weapons hit Los Angeles, the heart of America's entertainment industry and home to millions. The wall of fire triggered by the explosion was the largest that had ever swept across the Earth's surface—an inferno of biblical proportions that devoured everything in its path.

Within a radius of many kilometers, all life vaporized. People, animals, plants—nothing could withstand the unimaginable heat that for a brief moment reached the surface temperature of the sun. Concrete melted, steel vaporized, glass was blown into fine particles that later rained down on the surroundings as deadly, glass-like precipitation.

The atomic mushroom cloud reached a height

of sixty-four kilometers, pierced the stratosphere, and rose into the mesosphere. For comparison: The peak height of the explosion cloud of a nuclear weapon in the kiloton range is only a few kilometers. Even the largest thermonuclear tests of the 1950s and 1960s had not produced clouds that reached these dimensions.

The fireball had a diameter of seven kilometers—large enough to completely encompass Manhattan. This artificial sun illuminated the night like a second sunrise, visible over hundreds of kilometers. Pilots of commercial aircraft, who were at a safe distance, reported a brightness that penetrated even their tinted cockpit windows and temporarily blinded them.

Within a radius of thirty-five kilometers, everything was totally destroyed. No building remained standing, no tree upright, no road intact. The landscape was transformed into a moon-like desert, with melted rock and vitrified earth, where once thriving suburbs and busy business districts had stood.

Even at a distance of 270 kilometers, people still felt the heat radiation—a sudden, intense warmth, as if standing too close to an open fire. Window panes burst, easily inflammable materials caught fire, exposed skin suffered first-degree burns. The pressure wave reached these distant areas only minutes later, strongly attenuated but still strong enough to tear off roofs and overturn unsecured objects.

Europe, the USA, the major cities of China and Russia lay in ruins. What had once been the proud centers of human civilization were now smoking craters and radiating deserts. The infrastructure that had kept these complex societies alive—power lines, water supply, telecommunications, transport routes—was destroyed. The remnants of the modern world fell back into a pre-industrial age, only worsened by the omnipresent radioactive contamination.

The US President was dead. He had been in the bunker beneath the White House, the Presidential Emergency Operations Center (PEOC), which had actually been designed to provide protection to the President and his key advisors even in a nuclear crisis. Five floors below ground, reinforced with massive reinforced concrete walls and equipped with self-sufficient life support systems, it should theoretically have withstood a direct hit.

But theory and the cruel reality of modern nuclear weapons were far apart. When the capital was hit by Russian nuclear weapons—not by one, but by several—parts of the bunker ceiling collapsed. The President had been standing there next to one of the massive support pillars, because the security experts had advised him to—theoretically the safest place in the room. But the concrete ceiling caved in and buried him beneath it, along with the Vice President, the Secretary of Defense, and the

Joint Chiefs of Staff. The chain of command of the most powerful nation on Earth was beheaded in an instant.

Only the Secretary of State, who happened to be on a foreign trip, and the Secretary of Energy, who was inspecting an underground test site in Nevada, survived from the cabinet line. According to the American Constitution, they now became the highest remaining authority of the executive—leaders of a nation that barely existed anymore.

The Russians fired more nuclear weapons at Europe. After the primary military and urban targets were destroyed, they turned to secondary targets—smaller cities, industrial facilities, transportation hubs. It was as if a point had been crossed, beyond which there were no more inhibitions, no strategic considerations, only the desire for total annihilation of the enemy.

They also shot a tank corridor from Russia through Poland, Germany to Paris. Several dozen nuclear weapons struck like a string of pearls, to create a corridor—a broad swath of destruction that cut across Europe. The purpose of this nuclear path was to clear a route in case they would later send troops to Europe. A macabre "highway of death," lined with radiating craters instead of rest stops and gas stations.

In the entire NATO territory in Europe, there was not a single intact airport left. The runways were destroyed, the terminals transformed into piles of rubble, the hangars and control towers razed to the ground. The once busy hubs of international mobility had become radioactive deserts, their navigation systems and radar installations silenced forever.

In the USA and Canada, too, all airports had been destroyed. From the large international terminals like JFK, O'Hare, or LAX to regional airports and military air force bases—nothing had been spared. The air, once crisscrossed by the contrails of thousands of aircraft, was now empty, except for the ash clouds rising from the burning cities.

In the USA, there were only about fourteen cities with more than 100,000-200,000 inhabitants that remained undestroyed. Smaller communities in remote areas, far from strategic targets or larger metropolises, had survived—at least for now. Places like Boise in Idaho, Cheyenne in Wyoming, Missoula in Montana, or Flagstaff in Arizona became refuges for the few survivors who had managed to escape the death zones.

When the Americans learned of the destruction, the still living generals, who were in various bunker facilities or mobile command posts, urged to destroy even more Russian cities that were not militarily important. The logic of the "balance of terror," which had survived the Cold War, had now given way to blind vengeance. If America went down, so the thinking went, Russia should suffer the same fate.

And so the US Vice President, who now bore responsibility according to the presidential succession, although he was in a bunker beneath the Rocky Mountains, cut off from direct information and under extreme psychological pressure, gave the order to fire some nuclear weapons at still undestroyed Russian cities that were not militarily important. Places with rich history and culture like Yekaterinburg, Novosibirsk, Krasnoyarsk, and Irkutsk were selected—not because of their military significance, but as symbols of Russian identity and as home to millions of civilians.

As for EMPs, Europe had been lucky. EMP stands for "Electromagnetic Pulse"—an intense energy burst that can damage or destroy electronic devices and power grids. It occurs when a nuclear weapon detonates at high altitude, typically 30 to 400 kilometers above the Earth's surface. The released gamma rays collide with air molecules and generate a cascade-like stream of charged particles, which creates a strong electromagnetic field.

American Pegasus rockets, launched from specially modified F-15 fighter jets, had been able to destroy almost all Russian EMP satellites. This was the result of a years-long secret reconnaissance mission in which the positions and orbits of these satellites had been carefully cataloged. The Pegasus, a three-stage rocket that was originally developed for launching small satellites, was converted into an anti-satellite weapon that could strike with frightening precision.

But they failed to destroy one of those Russian EMP satellites as it passed over the North American continent. This satellite, disguised as an ordinary communications satellite, actually contained a compact thermonuclear warhead, specially optimized for generating a maximum electromagnetic pulse. When it was over the middle of the United States, it was remotely detonated.

It detonated and the electromagnetic pulse disabled electronics in large parts of the USA. It was as if an invisible tsunami swept across the country—not of water, but of pure energy. Electronic devices of all kinds were destroyed in an instant: computers exploded in a shower of sparks, phones melted in the hands of their users, power grids collapsed in a cascade of overloads, modern vehicles, packed with microelectronics, became useless lumps of metal.

The Russians had three such EMP satellites and the USA had two, since they would at most use them only against Russia and China, they didn't need so many. For countries with huge territorial expanses like Russia and the USA, the ability to detonate an EMP over a large part of the enemy's territory was a decisive strategic advantage. The effects were devastating: Not only were all electronic devices in the effective area destroyed, but also the infrastructure that would have been needed to repair or replace these devices.

The American EMP satellites, which were positioned over Russia, were activated before Russian ground defense systems could disable them. Two massive electromagnetic pulses swept across Russian territory, from St. Petersburg to Vladivostok, and disabled the remaining infrastructure in the largest country on Earth. What the direct nuclear attacks had not achieved, the EMP completed: Technological civilization was set back more than a century at a stroke.

Since the Russians' EMP satellite had detonated further north to also hit parts of Canada, there were still intact vehicles and electronic devices in parts of the southern states. In shielded military facilities, which had been specially constructed for protection against EMPs, some communication systems and basic infrastructure still functioned. But for the overwhelming majority of the population, the EMP meant the final collapse of modern civilization.

In Europe, the Russian satellite was supposed to detonate north of France. The Russians wanted to definitely target the two European nuclear powers—Great Britain and France—across their entire territories and neutralize their retaliatory capability. It was a cool, calculating strategy:

Eliminate the greatest threat first, then deal with the smaller problems.

But this third EMP satellite was destroyed by an American Pegasus interceptor rocket before it could reach its target. The rocket, fired from an F-15 fighter over the North Atlantic, hit the satellite with direct impact, shattering it into a thousand pieces. The nuclear warhead on board was damaged and did not detonate, a rare stroke of luck on this day of doom.

Thus, Europe was spared a wide-area EMP. Electronic devices continued to function, vehicles could still drive, communication systems still transmitted messages—albeit disrupted by the other effects of the nuclear conflict. It was a small victory amid a catastrophe of unimaginable magnitude.

CHAPTER 10: ARRIVAL

Meanwhile, the Thompsons arrived at the small harbor on England's west coast. After hours of driving along winding country roads, past panicking crowds and occasional military checkpoints, they finally reached their destination—the small fishing village of Porthleven in Cornwall, where David's brother Ben lived.

The evening sun hung low on the horizon, bathing the small bay in golden light. The rocky cliffs all around cast long shadows on the narrow sandy beach where children normally played and tourists sunbathed. But today the beach was deserted, the usual sounds of human activity silenced.

The village itself, with its narrow, winding streets and characteristic stone houses in white and pastel shades, appeared peaceful at first glance, almost untouched by the chaos reigning in the larger cities. But upon closer inspection, one could see the signs of crisis: barricaded windows, closed shops, and an unnatural silence that hung over the place like a heavy cloth.

Everywhere they saw cars, caravans, and occasionally some army vehicles. The small community, which normally counted only a few hundred permanent residents, was now overcrowded with refugees from the larger cities. Anyone who had connections to this remote coastal town—whether through family, friendship, or simply a vacation home—had flocked here, hoping to escape the nuclear inferno.

A rusty red tractor stood in the middle of the village square, next to it a fish transporter with an open loading area on which improvised sleeping places had been set up—blankets, sleeping bags, even an old sofa that someone had dragged from one of the houses. Some men had lit a campfire, around which women and children huddled, their faces eerily illuminated by the flickering firelight.

At the small fisherman's hut that served as an unofficial village hall, someone had hung a large banner with the words: "HELP EACH OTHER - WE ARE ALL THAT REMAINS." Underneath, some villagers had gathered, distributing tea from large thermoses and sandwiches prepared from the community's collected supplies.

The entire drive, since they had seen the atomic explosions, they had been afraid of radioactive fallout. Fallout, as it was technically called, was one of the most insidious dangers of nuclear war—invisible particles of death that could be carried by the wind for hundreds of kilometers, then slowly rain down to earth and contaminate everything they touched.

But with the wind blowing from the sea, they had been lucky. The clean air of the Atlantic kept the radioactive fallout away from them, pushing it deeper inland instead. It was one of those random strokes of luck that would later be remembered as the difference between life and death.

Nevertheless, they had considered stopping at a house somewhere and asking if they could take shelter in the basement. They had evaluated every tunnel, every bridge, every massive stone building as a potential shelter. But it hadn't been far to Ben's house, so David had raced his SUV along the country road, the gas pedal almost pressed to the floor, while the engine howled protestingly under the unusual strain.

David drove the car to his brother's house, which was located near the beach, not far from the mouth of a small river that wound through the hills before emptying into the bay. From his garden, there was a breathtaking view of the river, which lay only about 150 meters away, and of the gentle hills behind it, stretching like green waves to the horizon.

The blue house with gray roof tiles was still quite large for a fisherman's house. It was an old building from the 19th century, originally built as a harbor master's office and later converted into a residence. The thick stone walls, which had once withstood the rough Atlantic storms, were now painted white, almost seeming to glow in the evening light. The shutters were painted in a lighter blue, giving the house a maritime character, fitting for its location by the sea.

He stopped the car in the driveway, which was covered with pebbles. The crunching of the tires on the loose surface was a familiar sound that evoked memories of more peaceful times—of summer vacations, shared Christmas celebrations, of the time before the world went up in flames.

"Well, let's hope Ben is there," said David with a voice that, despite his efforts to sound calm, trembled with exhaustion and tension. He turned off the engine and leaned back briefly, eyes closed, to find a moment of calm after the strenuous journey.

Eva placed her hand on his, squeezed it gently in a gesture of wordless understanding. They were at the end of their strength, physically and emotionally drained from the strains of the escape and the horror of what they had seen.

They got out of the SUV. The salty sea air filled their lungs, a refreshing contrast to the stuffy atmosphere in the vehicle. The wind carried the rhythmic sound of the surf to them, a calming, timeless noise that stood in strange contrast to the apocalyptic events of the day.

Tim and Emma climbed stiffly from the back seat, stretched their tired limbs, and looked around curiously. For Tim, it was an adventure, despite the danger and horror. His childlike resilience allowed him to see the positive—a new place, the sea, his uncle's house. Emma, on the other hand, bore the knowledge of the catastrophe more heavily. Her eyes, normally full of joie de vivre, were now darkened by the images she had seen —the mushroom clouds, the crashed bomber, the crushed corpse on the road.

David hurriedly went to the entrance door, a massive wooden construction with wrought iron fittings that gave the house something castle-like. He rang the bell, the shrill tone of the old electric bell echoing through the house.

But no one opened. David knocked on the door, his knuckles hitting hard on the old wood, and rang again. The seconds stretched into eternity as they waited for someone to open the door.

"Maybe they're not there?" said Eva worriedly, looking through a long, frosted glass window right next to the door, which only revealed blurry outlines of the interior. Her voice trembled slightly, betraying her growing fear. What if Ben and Sandra weren't here? Where would they go then?

Then she saw a shadow coming to the door— a dark figure moving through the hallway. The sound of several locks being unlocked reached their ears, followed by the metallic click of a bolt being pushed back.

The door opened a crack, secured by a massive chain. A single, watchful eye peered through the gap, suspicious and tense. Then it widened in recognition, and the door closed briefly to remove the chain.

When it opened fully, David's brother Ben stood before them. He was the older of the two brothers, about 50 years old, with a weather-beaten face framed by a thick, graying beard. He wore worn blue jeans and a checkered flannel shirt with rolled-up sleeves revealing strong, work-marked forearms.

"David, good to see you. I'm so glad you're alive," said Ben, his voice breaking with emotion. He stepped aside and invited them in, opening his arms for a hug that David gratefully accepted.

The brothers held each other for a moment, in a silent communication that required no words. Despite their different life paths—David in the pulsating London financial world, Ben as a carpenter in this sleepy coastal town—they had always maintained a deep connection. In moments like these, the differences no longer counted, only the shared origin, the shared blood.

"Yes, we were lucky. We managed to get out of London in time," said David as they separated. His voice trembled slightly as the tension of the last hours finally subsided, now that they were in relative safety.

Ben also hugged Eva, who had tears in her eyes—tears of relief, exhaustion, but also grief for the world they had left behind. Then he knelt down to meet Tim at eye level and shook Emma's hand.

"We're in the cellar," Ben explained as he led them into the house. The hallway was dark, illuminated only by a few candles standing in holders on the wall. "You know, because of the radioactive fallout. But we're lucky, there's still no increased radioactivity here," he added, holding up a small Geiger counter that he carried in the pocket of his jeans.

The device, a compact model with a digital display, was one of the last that Ben had managed to obtain from the local yacht store before panic broke out and the shelves were emptied. He had bought it when tensions between Russia and the West began to escalate, more out of a vague premonition than out of genuine conviction that he would ever need it. Now it had become a life-saving tool.

"Do you still have room?" asked David, looking around in the semi-darkness of the hallway. The power had obviously failed, and the house seemed strangely quiet without the usual electronic background noises—no refrigerators humming, no air conditioners whirring, no televisions flickering.

"Yes, always for you. Of course, come in," said Ben without hesitation, a warm smile brightening his bearded face. Since he and his wife Sandra had no children, they lived alone in the large house that was actually designed for a family. "Good, I'd say we quickly get the things from the car into the basement. I've got more supplies with me," he added, pointing toward the kitchen where several boxes and crates were stacked—their own emergency supplies that they had collected in recent days.

"That's good. The children can go down to the cellar," Ben suggested.

They hurried to the car and hastily unloaded the things. The suitcases, bags, food supplies, and camping equipment were passed along in a human chain—David took them from the overcrowded trunk, handed them to Eva, who passed them to Ben, who carried them into the house. It went quickly, and the items were in the house. Ben's wife Sandra, a slim woman in her forties with short, blonde hair and a friendly but exhausted face, then helped move the things down from the house into the cellar.

Meanwhile, Emma and Tim went down to the cellar. The cellar stairs, a wide wooden construction that creaked slightly under each step, led down to a surprisingly spacious room. Tim held Emma's hand tightly as they carefully descended the steps, guided by the faint light of a battery-powered lantern that stood at the foot of the stairs.

The cellar was quite large. It actually consisted of just one large room, whose walls were made of rough, unhewn stone—a testament to the age and solid construction of the house. The low ceiling, supported by massive oak beams that had survived the centuries, seemed to press down on the room, giving it something cave-like.

The air was cool and damp, with a slight smell of earth and the sour aroma of stored apples. In one corner was a small, partitioned room containing the heating boiler and the oil tank—modern additions to this otherwise timeless place.

A wide wooden staircase led down, its worn steps testifying to generations of feet that had gone up and down here. In one corner was a workbench with some equipment and tools—Ben's refuge when he tinkered with his woodwork. The walls were lined with shelves on which neatly sorted tools lay: saws of various sizes, hammers, screwdrivers, pliers, drills, and countless other utensils whose purpose remained a mystery to the children.

Next to it stood the washing machine, a modern, white appliance that looked strangely out of place in this archaic environment, and a dryer that was placed on top to save space. Wooden shelves had been set up, looking older, with boards of dark, thick wood, on which things were stored—winter clothing in plastic boxes, Christmas decorations, old photo albums, sports equipment, and other relics of a normal life that had suddenly receded into the distance.

There was also a shelf with canned provisions that Ben and Sandra had accumulated in recent weeks as tensions between the superpowers increased—cans of beans, tuna, vegetables, and fruit, jars of pickled goods, packages of rice, pasta, and other staple foods that were long-lasting.

They had brought down the mattresses from the bedrooms and laid them on the floor, covered with sheets, blankets, and pillows—a makeshift sleeping place for the coming days or weeks they would have to spend down here.

The power had failed. Due to the electromagnetic pulses generated by the nuclear weapons, power grids nationwide had failed. The explosion of nuclear weapons at high altitude had released a massive electromagnetic pulse that swept across the country like an invisible tidal wave, destroying all unprotected electronic devices.

Many power plants had also been destroyed and the transmission networks destroyed, victims of targeted attacks on infrastructure. Without electricity, the pumps that pushed water through the pipes stood still, heating systems no longer worked, communication systems were dead. Modern civilization, so dependent on a constant flow of electrical energy, had been thrown back into a pre-industrial age within minutes.

Fortunately, the Americans had managed to shoot down the EMP satellite that was supposed to detonate over Europe with a Pegasus rocket, otherwise virtually all electronic devices and cars across Europe would have been destroyed. The Pegasus, a three-stage solid-fuel rocket fired from a modified F-15 fighter jet at high altitude, had hit the Russian satellite shortly before its planned detonation and shattered it into a thousand pieces, safely detonating its nuclear warhead in space where it could do no harm.

Unlike in the 70s, when many vehicles didn't contain much electronics and many vehicles would have survived an EMP, it was different in the modern computer age. Every modern vehicle was packed with microchips and electronic control units—from engine management to brake control to airbags and air conditioning. All this sensitive electronics would have been destroyed by an EMP in an instant, the semiconductors burned out, the integrated circuits melted.

Apart from special military vehicles equipped with Faraday cages and other protective devices, not a single vehicle would have driven after an EMP. The few remaining functional means of transport would have been vintage cars from a time when cars were still mechanically rather than electronically controlled, as well as bicycles, horse-drawn carriages, and other relics of earlier times.

The Russian EMP satellite that had detonated over the USA had not only destroyed almost all electronic devices in the USA but also most vehicles. Since the EMP satellite had detonated further north there to also hit parts of Canada, there were still intact vehicles in parts of the southern states. But even there, only about 10% of vehicles were still functional—mainly older models or those that had happened to be in metal buildings or tunnels that had acted as improvised Faraday cages.

In Europe, the satellite was supposed to detonate north of France. The Russians wanted to make sure to hit the two European nuclear powers across their entire territory. Great Britain and France, with their own nuclear deterrents, were primary targets for such an attack, aimed at neutralizing their retaliatory capabilities before they could deploy their own nuclear forces.

Ben closed the heavy wooden door to the cellar and placed a narrow cabinet in front of it—an additional barrier against possible radioactive particles that could enter the house. In the cellar, candles of various sizes and shapes burned, placed on shelves, tables, and the floor, their flickering flames casting dancing shadows on the stone walls.

An LED lantern also provided light, its cool, bluish brightness a stark contrast to the warm, golden glow of the candles. The lantern had a crank on the side and a small solar panel on top. This way, the lantern could be charged either with sunlight or by manual cranking—a sensible precaution for times like these when normal power supply had collapsed.

"We can get one or two more mattresses from the guest room," Ben suggested after they had brought all the supplies and luggage into the cellar. He wiped the sweat from his forehead, his face reddened from the exertion.

David nodded. Since there was still no increased radiation detectable, thanks to their luck with the wind blowing from the sea inland, they could still venture upstairs for short excursions. Depending on wind strength and direction and the strength and height of the nuclear weapon, the fallout zone could reach more than 100 kilometers from the explosion site. While against the wind it was often only a few kilometers where the radioactive radiation of the fallout was life-threatening. The wind was their luck—a random grace of nature that could decide between life and death.

Ben and David went up to the guest room and each took a mattress from the bed. The guest room, located on the first floor, was a cozy room with slanted ceilings and a small skylight through which one could see the sea on clear days. Measured with a double bed covered with a quilted bedspread in navy blue, an antique dark wood wardrobe, and a small desk under the window. On the walls hung watercolors by local artists depicting scenes of the Cornish coast—lighthouses, fishing boats, stormy seas.

"Have you heard from Dad and Mum?" asked David as they lifted the mattress from the bed. Their parents lived about a hundred kilometers north, in a small village in Devon, where they had settled after their father's retirement from his job as a teacher.

"Mum called this morning. Because of the nuclear war danger," Ben replied, his face darkening at the memory. "But after the first atomic bombs exploded, the phones went out too. I tried to call them, but the line was dead. I think they're sitting at home in the cellar."

David nodded, trying to show confidence that he didn't feel. "Do you know if they have many supplies?" he asked worriedly. He knew that after a nuclear war, one should not leave the shelter for two to three weeks to avoid radioactive fallout, whose intensity decreased over time. The most dangerous isotopes often had the shortest half-lives, which meant that the deadliest radiation would decrease to a less dangerous level after a few weeks.

"As far as I know, they bought a lot of supplies when tensions increased. You know Mum, she's immediately concerned about everything," said Ben with a slight smile that didn't quite hide his concern for their parents.

Their mother, a practical woman who had learned about two world wars through the stories of her own parents, had always insisted on having a well-stocked pantry. "You never know what's coming," had been one of her favorite sayings, and in this case, her caution had proven life-saving.

David and Ben went back down to the cellar with a mattress each. The stairs creaked under their weight, the old wood protesting against the unusual load. They laid the mattresses down on a free spot on the floor, next to those already there.

Eva was just telling Sandra what they had experienced. About the crashing bomber they had seen, and also about what had happened on the highway when they had driven over the corpse. She cried as she told this, the aftermath of shock finally breaking through now that the immediate danger was over. Sandra held her hand and tried to comfort her, although there were no words that could mitigate the horror of what they had experienced.

Eva still couldn't believe that London was gone. The city where she had spent her entire life, where she had given birth to her children, where she and David had met—all gone, wiped out in a fireball of unimaginable heat and destructive power.

Ben and David went upstairs again and brought more blankets and pillows. They moved more efficiently now, having become accustomed to the darkness and knowing the way. They had covered the windows of the house with cloth sheets to prevent any light from escaping—a precaution against potential looters looking for easy targets in the darkness.

They placed the bedding on the mattresses, carefully folded despite the chaotic circumstances. Maintaining order, even in small things, helped to preserve a sense of normalcy in a world that was anything but normal.

"I still have air mattresses here," said Ben and pulled two folded rubber mattresses from the shelf, still in their original packaging. He had bought them for camping trips some years ago but never used them—another example of how random possessions could suddenly become valuable resources.

David took them and immediately began to inflate one of them. The manual pump squeaked softly with each thrust, a rhythmic sound that was strangely calming.

"I hope we're lucky and the wind doesn't turn," said Ben, looking thoughtfully at his Geiger counter. The small device showed normal background radiation—about 0.1 microsieverts per hour, a completely harmless value. But they all knew how quickly that could change if the wind turned and carried the radioactive fallout to them.

"Yes, but here the wind often comes from the sea. It has to do with the Earth's rotation. Due to the Earth's rotation, the wind mostly blows from the west," explained David, while methodically continuing to inflate the air mattress. The Coriolis force, a consequence of the Earth's rotation, influenced global wind patterns, steering winds to the right in the northern hemisphere and thus creating the prevailing westerly winds in the middle latitudes.

"You were always the smarter one of us two," Ben grinned at his brother, a brief flash of the old, brotherly teasing that for a moment made them forget the grim reality of their situation.

David smiled back, grateful for this moment of normalcy. "Oh, I just read it somewhere. In one of my science magazines," he said modestly.

David continued to inflate the first of the air mattresses until it was plump and firm. The blue plastic gleamed in the candlelight, the wavy surface casting strange shadows on the walls. He set it aside and began with the second.

Ben meanwhile went to the freezer that stood in a corner of the cellar. It was an older model, bulky and white, with a heavy lid that sprung open with a dull sound as he opened it. He shone a flashlight inside, the beam casting the frozen foods into a ghostly relief.

"All this shit is thawing since the power's gone," he cursed as he inspected the contents of the chest. The surface of the frozen foods was already slightly thawed, a thin film of water had formed. "I would say we first eat a lot of things that would otherwise spoil before we start opening the cans."

Food storage would become a science in itself in the coming days and weeks—a balancing act between consuming perishable foods before they became inedible and saving canned goods for the uncertain future that lay ahead of them.

Ben took out an ice bucket containing a half-thawed pack of strawberry ice cream. "Does anyone want ice cream?" he asked with a crooked smile, aware of the absurdity of the situation—here they were, hiding in the cellar while the world around them was in flames, and he was offering dessert as if it were an ordinary family evening.

"The children surely do. Right, Tim and Emma?" said Sandra, trying to bring a piece of normalcy to this surreal situation.

"Yes, I'll take a little," said Emma, her voice quiet and tired, but grateful for the distraction. The prospect of ice cream, a joy from more peaceful times, seemed to bring a small spark of hope back to her eyes.

"Me too," nodded Tim, who sat on his mattress, his teddy bear firmly in his arms. The little boy had adapted surprisingly well to the new situation, accepting the strange environment and the tense atmosphere with the resilience of childhood.

Ben handed the bucket of ice cream to Emma. As

she looked around questioningly for plates, Sandra pointed to a basket containing plates and cutlery—part of their hastily assembled kitchen equipment for the cellar. Unlike most other items they needed, they had dishes and cutlery in abundance, an almost ironic luxury given the basic needs that would go unmet in the coming weeks.

"Oh, we still have a cake here," said Ben suddenly and took a box from the freezer containing a frozen cake. It was a raspberry cake that Sandra had bought for the upcoming visit of a friend—a visit that would now never take place.

Emma went over and took some of the white ceramic soup plates from the basket and filled them with ice cream using a silver spoon. She passed the plates to the others, her movements mechanical, as if following a well-rehearsed choreography.

Ben meanwhile unpacked the cake, which was already thawed. The raspberries on top glistened wetly in the candlelight, first drops of meltwater collecting at the edge of the cake. With a long knife, its blade flashing in the flickering light, he cut the cake into equal pieces, each movement precise and controlled.

"Phew, the last ice cream. Enjoy it, there won't be any more," said David to his children, his voice heavy with the realization of what they had lost and what they would never have again.

The thought that it might be the last ice cream they would eat in their lives made David shudder slightly. A wave of sadness and loss overcame him as he began to grasp the consequences of the nuclear holocaust in all its magnitude.

Even if they survived, civilization as they knew it was gone. And with it the ice cream factories, supermarkets, pharmacies and medical factories, simply everything they had once taken for granted. The complex supply chains, global trade networks, industrial processes needed to produce everyday items—all of it had been destroyed, wiped out in a moment of collective madness.

The more complex something was, like cars or computers, the more likely it would probably take decades before there might be factories producing such things again. The auto industry had taken over a century to become what it was known as before the nuclear war.

Suppliers had been distributed all over the world, a complex network of specialized companies that contributed only a small but indispensable part to the finished product—electronic control units from Japan, plastic parts from China, steel components from Germany, software from the USA. Countless engineers who had needed a century to develop what had been seen as something completely normal—a car that started at the push of a button, a computer that could perform complex calculations in fractions of a second, a smartphone that had more computing power than the devices that had once taken humans to the moon.

That was all gone now. Those who might eventually start building cars again in decades or in a century will have to start almost from scratch. They will first have to build the machines and tools to then in turn build those machines and parts that make up a car. They will have to rediscover the lost knowledge, reinvent the production methods, rebuild the supply chains from the ground up.

The nuclear war had simply swept away within a day everything that was known as civilization. David estimated that it would probably take at least another century before there would be car factories again, and the first products would probably not be able to match what had already been available until recently—they would be primitive, unreliable, inefficient, but they would exist, and that would be a triumph in itself.

Civilization had been swallowed by the flames of the nuclear inferno. David knew his son would grow up in a world where none of that existed anymore—car and computer factories, internet and cinemas with new Hollywood blockbusters. All that belonged to the past, artifacts of an era that had ended so suddenly and completely that it was almost impossible to comprehend the full extent of the loss.

It was something that made him sad, a deep, existential pain that went beyond the immediate loss of human life. It was the grief for a civilization, for centuries of human achievements, for art and science, for culture and technology—all reduced to radioactive ash.

Ben meanwhile poured coffee from a thermos and handed a cup to David, Eva, and Sandra. The coffee was strong and black, its bitter aroma mixing with the scent of burning candles and the slightly musty smell of the cellar.

He had taken a piece of the strawberry cake on a plate and sat down on a rickety wooden chair that creaked slightly under his weight. "The cake tastes good. It's not completely thawed yet, but you can eat it," he said between two bites.

The small group ate in silence, each lost in their own thoughts. The contrast between the sweetness of the dessert and the bitterness of their situation was almost too much to bear. Yet there was something comforting in this shared meal, in the routine of eating, in the shared experience.

"We should make a plan of which supplies to eat first," suggested David after he had drunk the last sip of his coffee. The cup was made of thin porcelain, decorated with a fine floral pattern—a delicate, fragile thing in a world that had suddenly become so hard and merciless.

"Well, I would say we eat all the fresh stuff first.

What will spoil soon," said Ben, as he pushed the last bit of cake from his plate. "The frozen things will thaw quickly, and most of it doesn't keep long. Then the things from the refrigerator, then the more durable foods like bread, fruit, and vegetables. We save the canned goods for later."

It was a logical approach, but it underscored the grim reality of their situation—they now had to plan every bite, every sip as if they were participants in a perverse survival game.

"How much water do you have?" asked David worriedly. Water was the most important thing—a human could survive weeks without food but only days without liquid. And in a world without functioning waterworks or electric pumps, every drop would be precious.

"What you see there," answered Ben, pointing to a corner of the cellar where six-packs of water bottles were stacked on top of each other. There were about twenty packages, each with six one-and-a-half-liter bottles—enough for a small group for a few weeks if they used it sparingly.

"We should fill the bathtub. Maybe there's still pressure in the pipe, even if the power is out," suggested David, an idea that suddenly came to him. The urban water systems often worked with gravity and pressure, which could be maintained for a time even without electricity, especially in areas where the reservoirs were higher than the consumption points.

"Good idea," Ben agreed and put the plate away. "And we should, if the water is still there, fill as much as possible. In buckets, pots, plastic tubs, just anything we can find. Not only for drinking and preparing food but also to be able to wash ourselves."

The limitations of daily life that lay ahead became increasingly clear. No more showers, no more toilet flushes, no more washing machines—all the little amenities they had taken for granted were now luxury. Personal hygiene, once a routine, would become a carefully planned operation, each drop of water precious and used with consideration.

They looked at each other and nodded, a silent agreement between survivors who were beginning to learn the rules of this new, harsh world.

Ben, David, Eva, and Sandra went up to the house. The stairs creaked under their feet as they ascended in a line, their movements careful in the semi-darkness. Once upstairs, they felt their way through the hallway to the bathroom, which was in the back part of the house.

The bathroom was small but functional, with a freestanding bathtub on claw feet, an old-fashioned washbasin, and a toilet with a high-hanging flush tank. The tiled walls, once white, had taken on a slightly yellowish tone over the years, and the floor was laid out with black and white tiles in a checkerboard pattern.

Ben tested if water still came from the tap. He turned on the faucet, and to everyone's relief, water came out, albeit at a lower pressure than usual. The thin stream splashed into the porcelain sink, a familiar, reassuring sound in a world that was becoming increasingly alien.

He rinsed out the bathtub, whose enameled surface was slightly cracked but still served its purpose, and then began to fill it with water. The water collected slowly at the bottom of the tub, rising centimeter by centimeter as they watched impatiently.

Meanwhile, the others searched every corner of the house for containers they could fill with water. Eva found several large pots and bowls in the kitchen, while Sandra brought buckets and plastic containers from the storage room. David discovered an old rainwater tank in the garden shed, which was empty but clean and could hold about 50 liters.

They filled all these vessels with water, working silently and efficiently as if they had practiced this task a hundred times. The splashing of water and the occasional creaking of the floorboards under their feet were the only sounds breaking the silence.

When all the containers were filled, they carefully carried them down to the cellar, where Emma and Tim were waiting. The children had meanwhile set up their sleeping places, arranged the blankets and pillows as if they were preparing a tent for an overnight stay in the garden—an attempt to give this eerie situation a touch of adventure.

They placed the filled water containers along the walls, provisionally covering as many as they could to prevent dirt from getting in—with cloths, plates, and plastic bags.

"I suggest that, before we drink the water from the bottles, we only drink water that we have from the tap for the first four to five days," said David as he set down the last bucket. "Because until then, it's still perfectly consumable even unboiled."

It was a pragmatic decision—the tap water would soon stop flowing when the reservoirs were empty or the pressure decreased, so they should use it while it was available and save their bottled supplies for later.

They found his plan good, nodding in agreement. In this new world, every drop, every can, every bite counted. Nothing could be wasted, nothing taken for granted.

David then helped Ben set up a camping toilet—a simple but effective device consisting of a sturdy plastic seat with a bucket attached underneath. They placed it in the small heating room, which thus became an improvised bathroom. Privacy was minimal, only ensured by a hanging curtain, but it was better than nothing.

Since it was November, it was even colder in the

already cool cellar. The stone walls radiated a damp coldness that penetrated to the bones. While it was still relatively warm in the house, thanks to the fireplace that Ben had lit upstairs and into which he had pushed a lot of wood. The warmth of the fire had seeped through the floors and had kept the house bearable for a few hours.

Now they were still lucky, and thanks to the Geiger counter, Ben knew he could still stay there without danger. Since there were no larger cities and important war targets in the area, it was unlikely that an atomic bomb had exploded nearby. Smaller communities and rural areas were often spared, not out of humanity, but out of simple military logic—they were not worthwhile targets.

Fortunately, Ben still had a paraffin heater in the cellar, which he had used for his motorhome. It was a compact device that ran on paraffin and could give off considerable heat—enough to keep a small room at a bearable temperature, if not comfortably warm.

But he didn't have much paraffin left and cursed as he looked at the almost empty canister. "If we only turn on the heater for two to three hours a day, it should last about four weeks," Ben calculated, his face thoughtful in the candlelight.

Eva and Sandra looked at each other worriedly. Winter was approaching, and in Cornwall, although milder than the rest of Great Britain, it could still get bitterly cold. The moisture from the sea penetrated the bones, making the cold sharper, more penetrating. Without adequate heating, it would be an uncomfortable, perhaps dangerous winter.

"It will be enough," assured David, though he wasn't entirely convinced himself. "In two to three weeks, the radiation on the surface will be so low that one can go outside relatively safely. And you have plenty of wood, don't you, Ben?"

Ben nodded. As a carpenter, he always had a good supply of wood, both firewood for the fireplace and timber for his projects. Additionally, behind the house stood a small shed filled to the roof with driftwood that he had collected on the beach over the years—salted and dried, it burned with a lively, blue flame and gave off intense heat.

He knew that even if they were unlucky and the wind changed direction and blew radioactivity toward them, in two to three weeks the radiation would have subsided enough that they could even go outside. The most dangerous isotopes released during a nuclear explosion often had short half-lives—the more deadly the radiation, the faster it passed.

They decided not to go back up to the house for at least the next two and a half weeks to avoid any risk. They sealed the gaps of the cellar door with duct tape, an additional barrier against radioactive particles that could enter the house. For safety, they also placed a narrow cabinet in front of the door—less as a physical barrier, more as psychological insurance that no danger from outside would enter.

They made themselves comfortable, as best they could under the circumstances. The mattresses and air beds were padded with blankets and pillows, candles strategically distributed throughout the room to ensure even lighting, and the supplies neatly stacked on shelves, a reassuring sight for people who didn't know when they would see a filled supermarket again.

David was glad that his brother's cellar had no window openings. Windows were the weak points of any shelter, openings through which radiation could penetrate. Only the door to the house was a weak point here, hence the additional precaution with the cabinet.

He knew that people could be much better protected in very large blocks, in windowless basement rooms of large buildings, than in cellars of small houses. The thick concrete foundations and several floors above offered considerable protection against radiation. But they were here, in the cellar of a solid, old house, and that was better than many other alternatives.

Meanwhile, Eva and Sandra made a salad with the fresh ingredients that would otherwise spoil. They had set up a small camping table, a folding model with aluminum frame and weatherproof top. Sandra still had lettuce, peppers, onions, and tomatoes that she had bought the day before, when the world still seemed normal.

Eva cut the tomatoes, her movements mechanical, her gaze absent. The red liquid seeping from the fruits involuntarily reminded her of blood, of the crushed corpse on the road, and she had to swallow several times to suppress the rising feeling of nausea.

"Do you like a lot of vinegar? I'm just asking because Ben and I usually put a lot of vinegar on it," asked Sandra as she put the cut vegetable pieces into a large ceramic bowl.

"Oh go ahead, we like a lot of vinegar too," Eva replied, grateful for the distraction from her dark thoughts.

Sandra poured a good splash of vinegar into the salad bowl, followed by some olive oil and a pinch of salt and pepper. With a wooden fork and a spoon, she mixed the salad until each piece was evenly coated with dressing.

David was glad that they had made it out of London and to his brother Ben. The tension he had felt fell from him like a heavy burden he had carried for too long. Relieved at not having died in the flame inferno in London, he let out a slight, quiet sigh.

"Man, I can't believe it. This morning I was still in London, which no longer exists," he said, the words barely more than a whisper, as if he was afraid to invoke the cruel reality too firmly.

"Yes, these damn nuclear missiles make the war so damn fast that probably many who were still sleeping in the USA when it started, woke up in a totally destroyed world. Not even 30 minutes does such a cursed missile need from Russia to reach a target in the USA. From a submarine near the coast, only minutes," Ben replied grimly, his face hard in the flickering candlelight. He had always had an interest in military technology, had devoured books about missiles and submarines —knowledge that had now suddenly become frighteningly relevant.

They then ate salad, sandwiches with salami and cheese, and also some fruit and cake. They ate their fill, knowing that this could be one of the last substantial meals for a long time. The fresh food would spoil quickly, and they would have to switch to canned goods and dry food—nutritious, but with little variety.

After the meal, they cleared away the plates and washed them in a bucket with some of the precious water. Nothing was wasted, even the dishwater was poured into a separate bucket to be used later for the toilet.

Exhausted by the day's events, they lay down to sleep. The children were the first to fall asleep, Tim cuddled close to his sister, the teddy bear between them like a talisman.

The adults stayed awake a while longer, talking quietly so as not to wake the children, exchanging information, sharing fears, making plans. But finally, fatigue overcame them too, and one after another they sank into a restless sleep, in which explosions and fireballs haunted their dreams.

CHAPTER 11: FLIGHT AF4011

In the first eight hours, most of the nuclear war was already over. Most nuclear weapons had been fired, causing unimaginable destruction in a short time. The strategic targets had been hit, major cities reduced to rubble and ashes, military facilities destroyed. What followed was an aftershock of devastation—power outages, collapsing communication systems, panic, chaos, and the beginning of a radioactive darkness that would last for generations.

The NATO troops in Europe were no longer organized and were already disbanding. The chain of command had collapsed when command centers and headquarters were destroyed. Without clear instructions, without functioning means of communication, without supplies, and without clarity about their mission, the once proud armed forces disintegrated into unconnected groups.

There were many small detachments of former soldiers who were making their way on their own. Some tried to return to their families, others joined together to form improvised combat units, ready to secure their survival with armed force. They moved through a surreal landscape of ruins and devastation, through villages without electricity, through cities without order, through a Europe that had been thrown back into a pre-industrial age within hours.

Their enemy, hunger and radiation, lurked everywhere. The nuclear winter had begun—ash and dust in the atmosphere blocked sunlight, causing temperatures to drop, making the cultivation of food almost impossible. The food chains that had once fed millions of people had collapsed. No electricity meant no cooling, no preservation. The supplies in supermarkets and warehouses quickly became coveted resources, fought and died for.

Soldiers looted shops and populations. With their weapons, their training, and their discipline, they had a decisive advantage over the civilian population. They could take what they needed, could intimidate or overwhelm others. Military discipline, once iron and principled, eroded rapidly under the pressure of the new reality. Moral boundaries blurred when it came to bare survival.

Many people were shot by soldiers and others if they carried a lot of food. A sack of rice, a box of canned goods—that could mean a death sentence in a world where the next meal was uncertain. Looting, raids, robbery—all these crimes, once strictly punished, became normality. The thin layer of civilization that had covered the darker aspects of human nature had been burned away in the nuclear fire.

Passenger planes that were on their way to Europe could no longer find an intact airport in NATO territory. They circled helplessly in the sky, their fuel gauges steadily declining, their radio requests unanswered or replied to with desperate, chaotic messages. The pilots, confronted with a situation for which there was no emergency plan, had to make impossible decisions.

Switzerland, however, still had many intact airports. The neutral country had been spared from the direct nuclear strike. Its airports—Zurich, Geneva, Basel—were still operational, their runways undestroyed, their navigation systems functional. Like islands of normality in a sea of chaos, they attracted desperate pilots looking for a safe landing place.

But those airports were overcrowded. Hundreds of planes of all sizes and types had already sought refuge there. The taxiways were full, the terminals overloaded, the resources exhausted. Each additional aircraft would only worsen the situation, mean more mouths to feed, consume more fuel, occupy more space.

So the Swiss anti-aircraft began shooting down

passenger planes that tried to land in Zurich. The 35mm Oerlikon cannons, actually designed to protect Swiss airspace from military threats, were now directed against civilian commercial aircraft. The decision, as cruel as it might seem, was necessary from the perspective of the Swiss authorities—better a controlled shot down over less densely populated areas than an uncontrolled crash over the city.

The tarmacs were clogged, there was simply no more free space. Planes stood wing to wing, their engines silent, their passengers either still on board or already accommodated in makeshift camps. The air traffic controllers, exhausted and overwhelmed, tried the impossible—to create order in a system that was never designed for such an onslaught.

Again and again, one could see how a passenger plane hit by the anti-aircraft went down in less densely populated areas. The Swiss artillery aimed precisely, tried to hit the planes in such a way that they did not explode immediately but went into controlled gliding flight and came down in less inhabited areas. It was a calculated risk, a cruel compromise between the safety of those already on the ground and the lives of those in the air.

This was also the fate of Flight AF4011. The elegant A380 of Air France, the largest passenger aircraft in the world, had already passed Greenland when Paris disappeared forever in the fireballs of nuclear weapons. The pilots had lost contact with air traffic control, suddenly found themselves in a world without instructions, without landing destinations, without the usual infrastructure.

The A380, a technological masterpiece with a length of almost 73 meters and a wingspan of nearly 80 meters, was designed for intact airports with long runways and modern navigation equipment. It was never intended to operate in a post-apocalyptic world where improvised landings on damaged or overcrowded airports were the only options.

The pilots, experienced professionals with thousands of flying hours, had therefore set course for neutral Switzerland, hoping that there would still be intact airports there. It was a logical decision, based on the limited information available and the urgent need to bring the plane and its passengers safely to the ground before the fuel ran out.

There was no time to search. Every minute in the air consumed valuable resources, brought them closer to the point where an emergency landing would be the only option—a prospect that would have catastrophic consequences for an aircraft of this size.

Sandra Hopkins sat by the window. The 54-year-old retired teacher looked at the clouds below the plane, occasionally broken to reveal a glimpse of the European landscape below. She could repeatedly see huge flaming areas, the sight of which made her shudder. The black columns of smoke rising to great heights, the unnatural, circular patterns of destruction—she could not understand what she was seeing, but it filled her with a deep, instinctive feeling of fear.

Her 57-year-old husband Thomas was with her on a holiday flight to France. It was their thirtieth wedding anniversary, which they planned to spend there. They had planned to see this steel colossus, the Eiffel Tower, which was once built in Paris at the end of the 19th century for the World's Fair there, and about which many Parisians cursed at the time because in their opinion it ruined the cityscape.

It was planned to dismantle the Eiffel Tower after the World's Fair, but it was left standing, and over time it had become the symbol of the capital of France. Lovers from all over the world felt magically attracted to that colossus of steel, which is held together by millions of rivets. With its curved shape somehow also reminiscent of a giant phallus. It couldn't be missing from any holiday photo from Paris.

They had specifically reserved a place in one of the restaurants on the first level, had looked forward to the view over the city, to the champagne they would drink there, to the shared remembrance of three decades of marriage. Now they would never see the city they wanted to visit—Paris no longer existed, the Eiffel Tower reduced to a bent skeleton, a grotesque sculpture in a nuclear desert.

The plane had started in New York, crossed the Atlantic, and was now in European airspace. It had taken off gently, gone into a slow climb, and the passengers had been gently pressed into their seats by the acceleration forces. A routine that took place thousands of times daily around the world—until this day.

During takeoff, Sandra had firmly squeezed her husband's right hand. Her hand was wet with sweat, for she was afraid and nervous, as always when flying. She had a fear of flying, an irrational but powerful feeling that haunted her during every takeoff and landing. The idea of flying in a metal cylinder through the air, thousands of meters above the ground, had always filled her with discomfort.

She had looked lovingly at her husband, who responded with a reassuring smile. They were a well-coordinated team, knew the small fears and weaknesses of the other, knew how to provide comfort, how to calm.

"Don't be afraid. Nothing will happen," he had said and smiled at her lovingly. His words, so often spoken over the years, had always given her security. But this time, without their knowing, they were a tragic irony.

The plane had set course northwards. It was supposed to go over Greenland and Ireland and then to France. An established route, flown thousands of times, refined and optimized for efficiency and safety. But no route had factored in a nuclear holocaust, no flight planning had considered what would happen if the destination suddenly no longer existed.

As the A380 approached Switzerland, the pilots were already informed about the catastrophe that had unfolded. Fragmentary radio messages from other planes, desperate messages from still functioning ground stations, their own observations from the air—all this had painted a picture of the horror that had befallen the world below them.

They had chosen Zurich as an alternative destination, hoping to be able to land there. Zurich Airport, one of the largest and most modern in Europe, seemed the best option in a world where options were rapidly dwindling. The pilots had communicated with the control tower, had asked for landing permission, had pointed out the urgent need to bring the plane safely to the ground.

But the answer was negative. "Airport overcrowded. No more capacity. Landing not possible." The words, sober and definitive, had sealed the fate of flight AF4011.

The Swiss authorities, confronted with an impossible situation, had made an impossible decision. The anti-aircraft batteries surrounding the country received the order to intercept incoming planes and bring them to a controlled crash—a cruel but, from their point of view, necessary measure to prevent greater catastrophes.

Shortly after the A380 had entered Swiss airspace, it was targeted by the anti-aircraft. The pilots, professional to the end, tried to evade, tried to initiate countermeasures, tried the impossible.

It was in vain. The anti-aircraft hit the right wing, tore a hole in the structure, allowed fuel to escape, which immediately ignited. And the bullets also hit one of the engines, destroyed it in an explosion of metal and fire. The plane staggered, lost altitude, went into a spin.

Panic broke out in the cabin. Oxygen masks fell from the ceiling, luggage tumbled from the compartments, people screamed, prayed, cried. Sandra and Thomas, still hand in hand, looked at each other one last time, their gaze a mixture of love and horror.

The plane crashed in a remote valley, about twenty kilometers east of Zurich. The impact was devastating, the plane broke into a thousand pieces, fire spread, consuming what remained. There were no survivors.

It was just one of many planes that crashed that day, just a fraction of the millions who died in the nuclear firestorms. But each lost life was a world unto itself, a collection of memories, hopes, dreams, loves—all extinguished, irretrievably lost.

In the days and weeks after the nuclear war, the wreckage of hundreds of planes would be found—in fields, forests, mountains, lakes. Silent witnesses to a global tragedy that claimed more lives in a few hours than any war before in the history of mankind.

Death toll at 11 PM: Worldwide: 683.2 million. But many severely injured who would not survive the next hours and days—victims of burns, radiation, injuries, hunger, thirst, and despair. The number of dead would continue to rise, would still increase weeks, months, years later, as the long-term effects of radiation, nuclear winter, and the collapse of civilization took their toll.

CHAPTER 12: THE DARKNESS UNDERGROUND

David lay awake on the air mattress, which rustled softly under his weight. Beside him, Eva breathed in shallow, regular breaths. Her face, only faintly illuminated by the flickering candlelight, looked more peaceful in sleep than during waking hours. He envied her this brief escape from reality.

The cellar room smelled of damp earth, of the musty dust of old shelves, and of the acrid note of the petroleum stove, which they only lit for a few hours a day. The roughly hewn stone walls seemed almost to pulsate in the dancing light of the candles, which were distributed at various stages of burning in safe places around the room. Their flickering flames cast ghostly shadows that crawled across the ceiling and walls like living creatures.

David couldn't sleep. His thoughts circled like birds of prey, always returning to the same tormenting questions. Would the wind continue to blow from the sea and keep the radioactive particles away from them? How long would their supplies last? Would they survive this nuclear winter?

His gaze wandered to the sleeping children. Tim had cuddled up close to his sister, his teddy bear wedged between them like a protective talisman. Emma's face twitched in her sleep. Was she dreaming of the world before the fire, of her school, her friends—all the things that were now lost forever?

He knew that they were relatively safe in the cellar of Ben's house, safer than many others at least. The strong westerly wind that swept over Cornwall from the Atlantic had so far kept the radioactive cloud away from them—their unexpected good fortune amidst the global inferno. But how long would this luck hold? A simple weather change could mean that deadly fallout would rain down on them.

David rubbed his tired eyes. In the cellar of a small house, one was far from being as well protected as in the deep cellars of large building complexes. The massive concrete blocks of high-rise buildings, the several floors above the cellar, offered far better protection from deadly radiation. But they had had no choice. His brother's house was their only option.

At least the cellar had no windows. These weak points in the defense against the invisible threat would have put them in even greater danger. He was grateful for the thick, old stone walls that surrounded them. They weren't perfect, but better than nothing.

A movement in the semi-darkness made David prick up his ears. Ben crept for the hundredth time to the cabinet that stood in front of the cellar door and pulled his Geiger counter from his pocket. The small device with its digital display had become their most important ally, a technological eye that could look into a world invisible to human senses.

"What does it say?" whispered David, so as not to wake the others.

Ben turned to him, his bearded face half in shadow. "Unchanged. About five millisieverts. More than normal, but we won't die from it." He put the device back in his jacket pocket, where he always kept it handy. "At least not right away."

This last, muttered remark was supposed to be a joke, but neither of them laughed. They both knew that long-term radiation exposure carried its own dangers—cancer, genetic damage, a slow, creeping death instead of a quick one.

"Some things you never get used to," said Ben quietly and sat down on a low stool next to David's mattress. "Three weeks ago, I was still thinking about what color to paint the kitchen walls. Now I'm measuring hourly whether the air is killing us." He rubbed his neck, where the tension of the last few days had accumulated. "Crazy, isn't it?"

David nodded silently. Yes, crazy was the right word. Crazy how quickly the world could end. Crazy how one could go from being a successful investment banker to a cave dweller fighting for bare survival. Crazy how the entire human civilization—millennia of progress, of art, of science—could evaporate in a nuclear fireball.

"I'm worried about my parents," said David after a while. "Do you think they made it?"

Ben placed a hand on his brother's shoulder. "Mum and Dad are tough, you know that. Their house has a good cellar, windowless and deep. And Dad has always prepared for the worst case, as long as I can remember." A faint smile flitted across his face. "Remember his survival kit? As children, we made fun of it."

David smiled at the memory. Their father, a retired teacher with a healthy dose of paranoia, had always kept a backpack with survival equipment ready—for natural disasters, for power outages, for World War III. They had dismissed him as an overly cautious crank. Now he appeared to them as a wise prophet.

"We'll find out as soon as it's safe to go outside," said Ben and stood up. "Try to sleep, brother. Tomorrow is another day in hell."

With these less than encouraging words, Ben returned to his own mattress and lay down beside his wife Sandra, who murmured quietly to herself in her sleep.

David continued to stare into the darkness, listening to the different breathing rhythms of the sleepers and to the occasional cracking of the cooling petroleum stove. He thought of London, of their house in Croydon, which now probably stood in a radioactive wasteland—if it still stood at all. Everything they had built up, everything they were, reduced to ashes and memories.

Sometime, between tormenting thoughts and fleeting images of the horror they had experienced, David finally slipped into a restless sleep.

The next day—if one could even speak of a day in their underground refuge, where time had merged into an amorphous mass of waking hours and restless sleep—began with a terrible discovery: The crank radio, their only connection to the outside world, was no longer receiving any signals.

Ben knelt before the small device, turning the knobs, cranking energetically, cursing softly. "Nothing. Not even static." He slapped the radio with the flat of his hand, a useless gesture of frustration. "Damn it!"

"Maybe it's broken?" suggested Sandra, though they all knew that this wasn't the problem. The radio had worked until recently. It was the world out there that had fallen silent.

"No more stations. No more emergency broadcasts." Ben let the useless device sink and looked at the others who had gathered around him. "That means..."

"That doesn't mean anything," David interrupted decisively. "Maybe it's just temporary problems. Maybe they need to repair antennas or replace generators." He didn't want to say what they were all thinking: that perhaps no one was left who could broadcast. That perhaps the last remnants of organized government or military that had maintained the emergency broadcasts had also collapsed.

Eva swallowed hard, her eyes betraying panic that she tried to hide from the children. "What do we do now? We have no idea what's going on out there. We don't know if the wind has turned, if we're sitting in a radiation cloud."

Tim, who sensed the growing tension, snuggled up to his mother. "Is the radio broken, Mummy?"

Eva stroked his hair, which had become dull and greasy after two weeks without proper washing. "Yes, darling. But that's not so bad. We still have each other."

Ben glanced at his Geiger counter. "The radiation is a bit higher than yesterday, but still in a range we can tolerate. The wind still seems to be coming from the sea."

"Should we risk going outside?" asked Sandra. "Just

briefly, to see what's going on?"

"No," answered David and Ben simultaneously.

"The risk is too great," added Ben. "From what I know, fallout radiation decreases most strongly in the first two weeks. The most dangerous isotopes have short half-lives. The longer we stay down here, the safer it will be up there."

"But without the radio, we don't know if new bombs have fallen. If there's anything left out there at all," argued Sandra.

"That's exactly why we're staying here," said Ben firmly. "At least another week. Then we can venture a brief exploratory trip."

Emma, who had listened silently until now, suddenly spoke up. "I never thought I'd miss the sun." Her voice sounded thin, almost brittle, and in her sixteen years, she had never seemed so young and vulnerable as now. "Or the fresh air. Or the rain on my face."

A depressing silence followed her words. They all missed the world out there, the world they had taken for granted until it had perished in a nuclear inferno.

To break the oppressive mood, David suggested playing a card game. It was a desperate attempt to bring a piece of normalcy into their life underground. They had found a worn deck of playing cards that provided the children with at least a few hours of distraction.

As they played Rummy, they suddenly heard a deep rumbling from outside. Everyone froze, the cards forgotten in their hands.

"What was that?" whispered Eva, her eyes wide with fright.

Another rumbling, louder this time, made the ground beneath them vibrate slightly. Tim clung to his teddy bear, tears in his eyes.

"It sounds like..." began Sandra.

"Thunder," Ben completed her sentence. "It's a thunderstorm."

They listened intently, and indeed: The rumbling had the typical swelling and subsiding of a thunderclap, not the sharp, explosive quality of a detonation. After a few seconds, another thunder followed, closer this time.

"A thunderstorm," repeated David and laughed with relief. "Just a damn thunderstorm."

They all laughed, hysterically, liberating, as if they had just outwitted an executioner. Just a natural phenomenon, not a new attack, no further escalation of the nuclear holocaust.

Ben, who could no longer curb his curiosity, stood up. "I'll just have a quick look."

Before anyone could protest, he had pushed the cabinet aside and cautiously opened the cellar door. A gap of about ten centimeters was enough to get a glimpse of the ground floor. Through the cracks of the shutters, he could see raindrops pelting against the windows, illuminated by the flickering blue of lightning.

The Geiger counter in his hand suddenly clicked faster. Ben cast an alarmed glance at the display.

"Shit," he muttered and quickly closed the door again. His face was ashen as he turned to the others. "The rain. It's washing the fallout out of the air."

Eva put her hand over her mouth. "Radioactive rain?"

Ben nodded grimly. "The Geiger counter has risen significantly. Not life-threatening, but..." He looked over at the children, who were listening with wide eyes. "We're definitely staying down here. And the door stays shut."

The storm raged all night. They heard it above them, like an angry beast rattling at their prison. The patter of the rain, which would have had a calming effect under other circumstances, now made them shudder. Each drop brought radioactive dust with it, contaminated the earth, the house, the water.

David tried to imagine what it looked like out there. Was the sky still dark from the dust and smoke of the explosions? Had the nuclear winter already begun? He had read that after a comprehensive nuclear war, enough soot and dust would be hurled into the atmosphere to block solar radiation for months or even years. Temperatures would drop dramatically, crop yields would collapse, famines would follow.

Their supplies, which seemed generously measured, suddenly appeared frighteningly scarce to him. What would they do when they were used up? Where would new ones come from in a world where supply chains had collapsed, where perhaps nothing grew anymore?

These dark thoughts accompanied him into a restless sleep, in which he dreamed of burning cities and fields where black ash grew instead of wheat.

On the tenth day of their underground existence, a kind of routine had been established. They had become accustomed to the constant hunger, to the cold that crept into their bones despite the petroleum stove, to the lack of privacy and the primitive hygiene with rationed water. They had even become accustomed to the fear that was now a constant companion, like an additional heartbeat under their skin.

Life in the cellar had become a strange new normality. They no longer measured time in hours and days, but in meals, in candles that burned down, in the slowly dwindling amount of water and supplies. The memory of the world before the fire faded like a dream upon waking, unreal and unreachable.

Emma and Tim had stopped asking when they would return home. Sandra and Eva hardly talked about their previous lives, about their work, their friends, all the small and large plans they had had. These things belonged to another existence, to people they once were, in a world that no longer existed.

Only Ben remained steadfastly optimistic, or at least pretended to be. He insisted that they would not only survive but build a new existence. He spoke of vegetable gardens they would plant, of fish they could get from the nearby sea, of a small, self-sufficient community that would rise from the ashes.

"We've been lucky," he said on this tenth day, as they sat around the camping table eating oatmeal with some canned milk—a meal none of them would have noticed before, but which now seemed like a feast. "We're alive. We have supplies. The wind has spared us from the worst. And we have each other."

David nodded, though he couldn't share Ben's optimism. Yes, they had survived—so far. But the world they knew had been swallowed up in a flaming inferno. Civilization, technology, culture, everything that defined humans beyond mere survival, had been wiped out.

The time in the cellar felt like a small eternity to them. The cold and barrenness, sleeping on mattresses on the floor, was hard on everyone.

Yet the cellar was large, they were sure they had been quite fortunate. They had food, they weren't many, they had enough water for a while, and the radiation was in a non-life-threatening range.

However, they found the lack of radio broadcasts bad and depressing. This not knowing what was going on outside. What was still there of the world? Were there still atomic explosions, or had it already stopped?

"It's time for a special breakfast," David suddenly announced and brought out one of his bread tins. It was canned bread, which according to the manufacturer should last eleven years. He opened the can with a soft hiss, and the smell of fresh bread—or something that remotely resembled it—filled the cellar.

"So, today we'll have bread again," he said, hoping it would lift the mood.

"With jam?" asked Tim with a childlike hope that broke David's heart. In the old world, his son would never have asked with such reverence for something as mundane as jam.

"We still have some left, then that too," said Sandra and got a small jar of strawberry jam from the pantry shelf. It was one of the last, and they shared it like a precious treasure.

David tore open one of the butter powder packages that he had brought and poured the contents into a bowl. With some water from the bottle, he mixed it into a butter-like paste. It wasn't the real, creamy butter they had mindlessly spread on their bread before, but it would serve its purpose.

They enjoyed the bread as they had rarely done in their lives. Each bite was precious, each hint of sweetness from the jam a small miracle. David watched as Tim ate his piece slowly, holding each bite in his mouth for a long time, as if he wanted to preserve the taste forever.

Again and again, they had to think about how carelessly they had eaten bread with butter and jam in the past. Something that seemed so precious to them here. How many in England and the rest of Europe no longer had bread and butter. It was a terrible thought that rose in David. A thought that said so much about the world they were in.

A terrible, cruel world of scarcity, in which even the simplest buttered bread with jam had become something precious, luxurious. Fortunately, he had bought butter powder and canned bread. It was something that brightened the souls of those who were with him a little here in this moment. And he cursed inwardly, for the canned bread, not even half a kilo for about five pounds, had seemed expensive to him at the time. He regretted not having bought much more of it.

The bread wasn't as delicious as that from the baker, but it tasted good enough to bring joy. Fourteen cans of bread remained. They planned to keep them longer, to open one of those cans once a week. But David knew that in just three months, this small luxury would also be gone. The time until then seemed terribly short to him. Three months, at once a week not even half a kilo of canned bread.

"Just terrible," he murmured, without realizing it.

"What's terrible, Daddy?" asked Tim, who swallowed his last bite.

David forced himself to smile. "Nothing, darling. I was just thinking."

"About what?"

"About how good the bread tastes," David lied. He didn't want to burden his son with his dark thoughts.

At noon there was soup from a can again, because his brother Ben had a large supply of that, which he had once acquired out of concern about a nuclear war. They ate in silence, each lost in their own thoughts, the scraping of spoons on the plate bottoms the only sound in the cellar.

After the meal, they washed the dishes in a bucket with carefully rationed water. Every drop was precious, reused wherever possible. The dishwater was poured into a separate bucket to be used later for the toilet. Nothing was wasted, nothing taken for granted.

When the two weeks they had set as a minimum for their cellar stay had passed, they dared only a brief look through the door. Outside it was still raining. From the radio announcements, they knew that it had rained continuously for the first seven days.

"It's still raining. How long will the rain last?" said David as he peered through the narrow gap outside.

Ben shrugged. "No idea."

He measured the radiation with the Geiger counter. The display showed 4.2 millisieverts. High, but not life-threatening.

They decided to endure a few more days and only then go up to the house. They closed the door again, pushed the cabinet back to its place.

They stayed in the cellar for another five days.

They had long since lost their sense of time. Without their watches, they wouldn't have known whether it was day or night. They had also already started to ration the food they had more strictly. There were still plenty of supplies, but they would only last for about five months. They hoped that when they could go out again, things would get better. Perhaps help would also come through the ports. Food from countries of the world that were not affected.

Ben and David went to the door and removed the duct tape.

When they had removed it, Ben opened the door a crack and first held his Geiger counter outside to test.

"And how much?" asked Eva, who stood at the bottom of the stairs and looked up at Ben anxiously with Sandra and the children.

"3.7 millisieverts. So we can risk it," said Ben.

They were happy that it was so low—relatively speaking, of course. It was still almost forty times more than normal background radiation, but far below the range that would cause acute radiation sickness.

Ben said: "You stay down here for now. There might be hotspots with increased radiation in the house. I'll look around there first and then let you know."

To David, who wanted to come along, Ben said: "You stay here too."

David nodded and watched his brother as he went into the house, up the old wooden staircase that creaked under his weight as if it would give way at any moment.

A new world awaited them. A world after the fire. A world in which they had to learn how to start from scratch.

CHAPTER 13: AWAKENING

It was bitterly cold in the house. Breath formed small, ghostly clouds in front of Ben's face as he carefully crept through the hallway. His footsteps echoed on the old floorboards, an unnaturally loud sound in the deathly silent surroundings. The temperature outside was about fourteen degrees below the normal value for December—a consequence of the nuclear winter that had already begun.

The icy breath that penetrated through every crack made him shiver despite the thick wool sweaters he wore layered on top of each other. Ben rubbed his rough hands together, looking at the cracked skin with the split knuckles—a result of the water shortage and lack of skin care. Small things like hand cream, which one had carelessly used before, were now unattainable luxuries.

Ben knew the cause of the extreme cold. The countless atomic explosions had hurled unimaginable amounts of dust and soot into the Earth's atmosphere. The burning cities, the melted buildings, the charred forests—all had created a dense cloud of particles that now blocked the sun's radiation. Scientists had warned about this for decades. In the old documentaries about nuclear winters that he had seen, this consequence had always appeared as an abstract threat, a theoretical possibility. Now he was experiencing it firsthand, feeling the biting cold that penetrated not only his bones but his soul.

Almost everywhere in the house, the blinds were lowered, which intensified the already gloomy atmosphere. Thin strips of muted light penetrated through the cracks and drew pale lines on the floor. The shadows in the corners seemed almost tangible, as if they had gained their own substance in this new, hostile world. The familiar house, in which he had lived for years, suddenly seemed strange and threatening to him—a ghost house, caught between the old world and the new.

Ben walked to one of the windows in the living room. The heavy, jade-green velvet curtains hung motionless in the still air. Dust flakes had collected at the edges, glittering in the sparse light like tiny diamonds. With hesitant fingers, he pushed the curtain aside a crack and peered cautiously outside, as if he expected someone to be watching him.

What he saw took his breath away.

The garden, once his pride with carefully tended roses and neatly cut lawn, lay buried under a thick layer of snow. Half a meter at least, he estimated. In December, in Cornwall, where the mild Gulf Stream normally provided moderate weather. The fir trees at the edge of the property bent under the load of snow, their branches hanging so low that they touched the ground. In the distance, where the sea was normally visible, a dull, grayish fog veiled the view, as if the world beyond his garden had simply disappeared.

It was a sight of ghostly beauty—the untouched white snow, the complete silence, the diffuse light that bathed everything in an unreal shimmer. And yet it was at the same time an image of deep, existential threat. This snow was not the friendly white of a winter wonderland; it was the pale shroud that was spread over the dying world.

Ben turned away and walked further through the house, always holding the Geiger counter in front of him like a talisman. The radiation meter ticked softly, a disturbing sound that reminded him of a time bomb. The display fluctuated between 2.1 and 3.7 millisieverts, depending on where he was at the moment. The values were particularly high near the windows and by the chimney—places where radioactive particles could more easily penetrate into the house.

He went on to the kitchen, a cozy, maritime-styled corner with light blue cabinets and a massive countertop made of oak wood, on which traces of hasty digging could still be seen. Three open cans stood on the counter, their contents now moldy. They must have forgotten these in the rush when they fled to the cellar. The air smelled musty, with a hint of spoilage—the typical smell of a house that had remained uninhabited for too long.

Ben opened the refrigerator and immediately twisted his face. The pungent stench of spoiled food hit him. Without electricity, everything had turned into a putrid, slimy mass. He quickly slammed the door shut again and made a mental note to completely clean out the refrigerator later and disinfect it, if they even still had disinfectant.

He wandered further through the ground floor, checking each room with his Geiger counter, before finally taking the stairs upstairs. The steps creaked under his weight, a sound that had once been ordinary but now seemed supernaturally loud in the absolute silence of the house. He paused briefly, listened, as if expecting a response to the noise, but there was only the dead silence.

Upstairs were the bedrooms—the master bedroom he shared with Sandra, the guest room, and his study where he made his wood carvings. Up here it was even colder, as the heat in the house rose and escaped through the leaky roof. Ice flowers had formed on the windows, delicate patterns that shimmered in the diffuse light.

He systematically checked each room, always keeping an eye on the Geiger counter display. The values were consistently in the tolerable range, nowhere above 3.8 millisieverts. It was far more than the natural background radiation, but still far below the acutely dangerous values at which radiation sickness would threaten.

After his inspection of the upper floor, Ben was sure: The house was safe enough for all of them. They could move up from the cellar and lead a somewhat more normal life again— or at least as normal as was possible under these circumstances.

He went back to the ground floor and to the terrace door. This had a special significance for him; on sunny summer days, he had always opened it wide, had let in the warm wind and the scent of blooming roses. Here he had often sat with Sandra, a glass of wine in his hand, while they watched the sunset over the sea.

Now he stood before the same door, but the world behind it had fundamentally changed. With a deep breath, he opened the door a crack and held the Geiger counter outside. The small device immediately responded with a faster ticking. The display climbed to 4.2 millisieverts.

"Damn shit," muttered Ben and sharply sucked in the air.

Four point two millisieverts were significantly more than inside, but still not immediately life-threatening. It meant they could go outside for short periods—to do necessary work, to collect firewood. But it also meant that the threat was real, that fallout had actually descended here, in their little corner of Cornwall.

Ben stared at the display, which fortunately remained stable and did not rise further. A weight lifted from his heart. They could have been unlucky—an unfavorable gust of wind would have been enough to carry a deadly dose of radioactive dust to them. A few hundred kilometers to the north, in the industrial centers of Wales or the Midlands, which had most likely been direct targets, the Geiger counter would probably have hit so hard it would have become unusable.

He closed the door again, turned the key twice in the lock. Now that he knew it was relatively safe outside, he felt an irrational urge to erect every possible barrier between this irradiated outside world and his refuge.

With one last examining look through the house, Ben went back to the cellar door. He opened it and called down: "You can come up."

His voice, the first human voice in this house for over two weeks, sounded strangely hollow in the empty rooms. Almost as if the house itself no longer recognized it, as if it were surprised to harbor life in its walls again.

He heard muffled murmuring, then the scraping of feet on concrete as the others prepared for the ascent. David appeared first in the doorway, his gaunt face tense and alert, his eyes narrowed to slits as he adjusted them to the relative half-light of the house after the deep darkness of the cellar.

"Everything all right?" asked David, his voice no more than a whisper, as if he feared being heard by unknown enemies.

Ben nodded. "The radiation is elevated, but not dangerous. Between 2.1 and 3.8 millisieverts in the house, somewhat more outside. We can live up here as long as we don't spend too much time outdoors."

David audibly exhaled, a tension releasing from his body that he had held for so long he had hardly noticed it anymore. "Thank God," he murmured and stepped fully out of the cellar hole.

Eva followed him, the children close behind her. They were so glad to finally escape the oppressive confinement of the cellar. It felt so strange to be able to stand upright again, no longer constrained by low ceilings and damp walls. And yet there was a peculiar sense of unease in the air, as if they weren't sure whether this house—this piece of normality from the time before the fire—really still belonged to them, or whether they were intruders in a foreign world.

Tim held the small teddy bear tightly clutched, which he had kept with him the whole time in the cellar. His large, blue eyes wandered curiously through the room, taking in every detail, as if seeing it for the first time. In a way, that was true —the two-week cellar existence had so distorted his childlike sense of time that the memory of the house itself had faded.

"It's so cold," whispered Emma, her arms wrapped around herself, as she suppressed a slight shiver. Her normally lively, freckled face was pale and hollow, her cheeks gaunt, her eyes too large for her narrow face—traces of the meager diet and permanent stress of the past weeks.

Ben noticed the condition of the girl with a pang of concern. Children should grow up in safety, surrounded by warmth and abundance, not hide in cellars and tremble before invisible threats.

"We will make a fire," he said with a determination that he didn't really feel. "I have enough wood for the fireplace, and later we can get more from the forest."

Sandra, who came last from the cellar, nodded in agreement. "And we should bring up the mattresses. It makes no sense to leave them down there if we're going to live up here now."

Ben went to the fireplace, a massive structure of roughly hewn natural stones that dominated the western wall of the living room. The hearth, framed by a worn wrought-iron grate, still contained the charred remains of the last fire they had lit before their descent into the cellar—a gray, ash-covered reminder of warmer times.

He knelt down and filled the hearth with fresh logs, which he took from a woven basket next to the fireplace. The logs were dry and well-seasoned —Ben had always been proud of his carefully maintained wood reserve, a hobby that could now prove life-saving. Between the larger logs, he pushed crumpled newspaper and smaller wood splinters, then some of the grill lighters that he had bought for the garden barbecue.

With slightly trembling fingers—a combination of cold and nervous tension—he lit the paper with one of the few remaining matches. The fire caught immediately, small flames licking hungrily at the dry wood splinters, devouring the paper and attacking the larger logs. Within minutes, a lively fire crackled in the fireplace, casting dancing shadows on the walls and spreading a pleasant warmth that slowly began to dispel the icy cold in the room.

The smell of burning wood filled the room, a comforting, archaic scent that appealed directly to something primeval in them. Tim approached the fire like a moth to light, stretched out his small hands to feel the warmth. His eyes shone in the reflection of the flames, a rare moment of childlike joy in a world that had no place for children anymore.

While Ben tended the fire, the others set about bringing the mattresses up from the cellar. David and Eva carried two of them, while Sandra and

Emma carried the blankets and pillows. They laid everything out in the living room, close enough to the fireplace to benefit from its warmth, but far enough away to avoid any fire hazard.

They kept the blinds down. They only opened them a crack, just enough to let a little natural light into the rooms, without anyone outside noticing that the house was inhabited.

Eva went into the kitchen, which was connected to the living room by an open passage, and turned one of the water taps experimentally. There was a rasping sound in the pipes, a short gurgle, then silence. Not a drop of water appeared.

"Damn it," she said softly, but in the silence of the house, her voice carried further than intended.

"What's wrong?" asked David from the mattress, where he was just trying to smooth out the wrinkled sheets.

"No water," replied Eva with a resigned shrug. "The pumps probably don't work anymore without electricity."

It was no surprise, but still a hard blow. They had hoped that at least the water supply would continue to function for some time, as many systems worked with gravity and pressure. But apparently the reservoirs were already empty or the pipes damaged.

"Luckily we still have our water supplies in the cellar," said Ben, who by now had the fire under control enough to rejoin the conversation. "And if necessary, we can melt snow. We have plenty of that, at least."

David and Ben went to one of the windows that faced forward to the courtyard. They opened the blind a crack, just enough to peer out without being noticed from outside. The roadway in front of the house, normally used by only a few residents, was now completely parked with vehicles of all kinds—cars, motorhomes, even an old rusty tractor.

Several motorhomes stood close together at the roadside, their windows covered with improvised curtains—blankets, jackets, newspaper. From one of the chimneys rose thin smoke, a sign that people inside were also trying to defy the cold. In front of one of the campers sat a man on a folding chair, wrapped in a thick wool blanket, his face half hidden under a knitted cap. His skin looked unnaturally reddened and blotchy even from a distance.

"Radiation sickness," Ben murmured quietly as he observed the man who stared apathetically ahead. "He must have been in one of the more heavily affected areas before he came here."

David nodded grimly. He knew what that meant. The initial erythema, the reddening of the skin, was one of the first signs of radiation damage. It would not stop there. Soon nausea, vomiting, and diarrhea would follow, then hair loss and internal bleeding. Without medical care, without antibiotics and blood transfusions, death was inevitable. It was a cruel fate, and there was nothing they could do for this man.

In one of the neighboring houses, several houses away, they noticed busy activity. Several people moved inside, their silhouettes occasionally visible behind the only half-covered windows. In front of the house, others had lit a campfire over which a large cauldron hung. An improvised outdoor kitchen in which something was probably being cooked that deserved the name 'meal' only out of courtesy.

"People are organizing themselves," said David quietly. "That's good. Alone, one has no chance in this new world."

Ben nodded thoughtfully. "The question is just how they are organized. As a community that works together—or under a leader,"

CHAPTER 14: ARE THEY STILL ALIVE?

After the meal, David set out to visit his parents. To save fuel for the car—gasoline was now more precious than gold—he decided to cover the distance by bicycle. He took Ben's bike, a sturdy mountain bike with wide off-road tires that had been standing in the garage. The matte black aluminum frame was scratched and slightly dented in some places, but the vehicle was solid and reliable—exactly what he needed for this dangerous journey.

"Take care of yourself," said Eva as she said goodbye and hugged her husband tightly. She wore three sweaters on top of each other to defy the biting cold, and her thin arms felt unusually voluminous as she embraced him. Her eyes, sunken in dark hollows of exhaustion and worry, betrayed the fear she felt. In this new, lawless world, every trip outside was a game with death.

"I'll be back before dark," promised David and

kissed her gently on the forehead. Her skin was cold and dry, her once shiny chestnut brown hair dull and lifeless. The last weeks had taken their toll on all of them, had sucked the shine from their faces and left only shadows.

Ben, who leaned in the doorframe, an old muzzle-loading revolver in his waistband—an antique that he had inherited from his grandfather and for which he even still possessed half a dozen cartridges—nodded grimly. "Don't worry. We're careful."

He handed David a small flashlight, a compact LED light with an aluminum housing that still gave off a bright, focused light even after weeks without charging. "In case you don't make it back before dusk after all. The batteries are still good."

David put the lamp in the pocket of his jacket, a worn-out down jacket in dark blue, whose quilting was already thinned out in many places, but whose heat insulation was still sufficient for the short journey ahead of him. Over one shoulder, he threw a small backpack containing some water, a few energy bars, and a rudimentary first-aid kit—indispensable precautions in a world where every journey could potentially turn into an odyssey.

Tim, who had been watching the proceedings from the background, suddenly stepped forward. His small face was serious, the usual childlike carefreeness completely gone. He stretched out his hand, in which he held a small object—a toy figure, a superhero in a red costume, whose color had already partially flaked off. "Take this with you, Daddy," he said with the serious determination of a child who had to grow up too early. "It will protect you."

David went down on his haunches to be at eye level with his son and accepted the figure. It was Tim's favorite toy, a treasure from that distant time when the boy's biggest worry was still whether he would get a story read to him before bedtime. "Thank you, little one. But are you sure you can spare it?"

Tim nodded, his eyes wide and resolute. "It's magical. It watches over you."

A lump formed in David's throat as he pocketed the small plastic toy. It was so light, so meaningless in a material world—and yet infinitely precious as a symbol of the love and trust his son placed in him. "I'll take good care of it," he promised and hugged Tim tightly. "And I'll be back soon."

With these words, he swung himself onto the bicycle. The chain squeaked protestingly as he pedaled—the bike had stood unused in the garage for too long, the moving parts were dry and rusted. But it rolled, and that was all that mattered.

The first meters were the most difficult. After weeks, almost months of inactivity in the cellar, his muscles were weakened, his circulation sluggish. Each pedal push sent waves of pain through his thighs, and his breath came in bursts, forming small clouds in the icy air. But with each meter, it became a little easier. The body remembered the movement, found its way back into the old rhythm.

The road leading away from the house was covered with a thin layer of snow, which in places was compressed into ice. The tires of the mountain bike, however, found good grip thanks to their rough tread and wide contact surface. David rode slowly and carefully, watching for hidden obstacles and treacherously slippery spots.

The surroundings, once a picturesque coastal town full of life and color, had now become a ghostly landscape of snow and silence. The colorful fishing boats that normally bobbed in the harbor lay buried under a layer of ice or had long since disappeared—stolen, dismantled, used as firewood by those who were desperate enough to sacrifice everything for a bit of warmth.

The houses stood still and lifeless, many with broken windows, smashed doors, traces of hasty looting or desperate flight. Only from some rose thin trails of smoke, signs that someone was still holding out there, clinging to existence like to a breaking branch over an abyss.

David turned onto one of the main roads that led inland. Here the picture became even clearer. Burnt-out car wrecks partially blocked the roadway, forcibly pushed-aside vehicles formed a kind of irregular corridor. It looked as if someone —presumably the military or organized survivors —had cleared a passage to be able to pass with vehicles.

He rode along the streets, past abandoned houses and improvised accommodations. Everywhere he saw signs of collapse: broken windows, garbage on the streets, burnt-out car wrecks. But also signs of life and resilience: makeshift repaired roofs, small vegetable gardens in front yards where people desperately tried to grow something edible under the pale light of the veiled sun, improvised windmills made from old bicycle parts and plastic tarps that probably drove small generators.

At a street corner, someone had set up a makeshift market stand, a rickety structure made of old pallets and a plastic tarp. A shriveled old man in a dirty parka crouched behind it, his eyes watchful and suspicious under bushy gray eyebrows. In front of him on a board lay some dead rats, carefully skinned and gutted, next to them a pile of shriveled roots and a small stack of hand-rolled cigarettes—the new currency of the post-atomic war world.

The old man raised his hand in greeting as David passed by, but his other hand remained under the counter, where presumably a weapon was hidden. In this new world, mistrust was not only advisable but vital for survival.

David nodded briefly back but did not stop. He had nothing to offer for barter, and the starved looks of some ragged figures who were loitering near the stand told him that he was doing well to keep going. His bicycle alone was valuable enough to be attractive as robbery prey, not to mention his warm clothing and the backpack with the few supplies.

Again and again, he encountered refugees who had taken up quarters in empty houses. Many of the houses were overcrowded, three or four families crowded into rooms that were previously intended for just one. Through open windows and doors, he could look into makeshift living spaces where people slept on the floor, surrounded by the few possessions they had saved from their previous lives.

He also saw injured and sick people—people with burns, with cuts that had become infected, and above all frighteningly many blind people. They had looked into the nuclear flash, and the high-energy radiation from the explosions had burned their retinas, had taken their eyesight in a fraction of a second. They carefully felt their way along house walls, were led by children or other survivors, their gaze empty and absent, their faces often consumed by the radiation that had transformed their skin into a grotesque mask of blisters and open wounds.

A little girl, no older than his daughter Emma,

stood in front of a decaying row house and stared into the distance with empty eye sockets. Her skin was strangely blotchy, red and white patches alternating like a macabre checkerboard pattern. She held a worn teddy bear in her thin arms, whose fur was almost completely worn off. As David rode by, she turned her head in his direction.

"Do you have something to eat, mister?" she asked with a voice as thin as paper, as brittle as old glass.

David stopped, overwhelmed by pity and a deep, gnawing guilt. These children, these victims, they had done nothing to deserve this fate. They had simply been in the wrong place at the wrong time, victims of the power struggles and madness of adults.

He rummaged in his backpack and found one of the energy bars he had packed for emergencies. It was a simple bar of oats, dried fruits, and honey, sealed in plastic to keep it fresh. He handed it to the girl.

"Here, little one. But ration it carefully," he said quietly as he placed the bar in her outstretched hand.

The tiny fingers of the child closed around the gift as if it were a precious gem. A pale smile flitted across her face. "Thank you, mister," she whispered. "God bless you."

David swallowed hard as he got back on the bike. God. If there was a God, where was he when the bombs fell? Where was he when the children burned and the innocent died? These questions, which so many had asked since the event, had no satisfying answers.

He rode on, trying to banish the image of the girl from his head, but it had burned itself in, alongside all the other images of horror he had seen since the day of the fire. They would haunt him, probably until the end of his life.

David did his best to remain inconspicuous as he pedaled through this apocalyptic landscape. The road itself was mostly clear, but in some places abandoned vehicles blocked the way, and he had to dismount and carry the bicycle around the obstacles. The snow made progress additionally difficult; several times the tires slipped away, and he had to use all his skill not to fall.

He rode past the old stone church, surrounded by about three dozen houses and cottages, a pub on the main street and a small general store that offered the necessities for daily needs.

The church was still standing, its massive stone tower defying the elements as it had for centuries. But the pub had burnt-out windows, and the store had obviously been looted, its door hanging askew in the hinges, the shop windows shattered.

When David saw his parents' white wooden house in the distance, he breathed a sigh of relief. The house, a traditional English cottage with a thatched roof and a small, fenced front garden, looked undamaged on the outside. A thin column of smoke curled from the chimney into the gray sky. The blinds, which his father had installed years ago as one of his many precautionary measures, were lowered, and his father's car, a black, compact Land Rover SUV, was parked in the driveway—a good sign.

David got off the bicycle and pushed it the last few meters to the house. His legs trembled with exhaustion, and he felt a stabbing pain in his right knee, an old sports injury that was making itself felt again under the unusual strain.

He leaned the bicycle against the wall of the house, next to a neatly stacked pile of firewood—his parents had always been practical, had always kept a supply of everything that might be needed. A trait that David had often smiled at, but which could now prove life-saving.

With hesitant steps, he went to the door. He rang the bell first to announce his arrival—a strangely normal gesture in a world that had lost all normalcy—and then took the key that he had received from Ben out of his trouser pocket. The key was cold in his fingers, the metal almost painful on his skin after the long ride through the cold.

Time seemed to stretch as he inserted the key into the lock, turned it, and slowly, carefully opened the door. He was ready to close it immediately if something was wrong. The door swung open and revealed a dark hallway, where only sparse light penetrated through the cracks of the closed shutters.

"Mum, Dad, are you here?" he called loudly and listened attentively for an answer.

The house was filled with the same oppressive silence as Ben's house before—the silence of a place that had been too long without human presence. The slight creaking of the floorboards under his feet echoed unnaturally loudly through the deserted hallway. For a terrible moment, David thought that he might have come too late, that his parents might...

But then he heard a sound, a soft scraping, followed by the unmistakable creaking of the old wooden staircase that led to the cellar. It was a characteristic sound that reminded him of his childhood—how often had he heard this specific creaking when his father went downstairs late at night to get something from the storage cellar.

"David," he heard his mother call, her voice thin and shaky, but unmistakably hers.

Relief hit him with such force that his knees went weak for a moment. They were alive. They were here. In this world full of loss and despair, this was a rare and precious gift. David felt tears come to his eyes, and he blinked hastily to push them back. Not now. He had to be strong, had to function.

He went to the cellar door, his steps echoing on the old oak parquet of the hallway. From the half-darkness of the first room, he could only dimly make out the familiar objects of the parental house —the old oak sideboard with the Venetian mirror above it, the dresser with the family photos, the antique brass umbrella stand in which his father kept his collection of walking sticks. Everything was covered with a thin layer of dust, hidden as if under a gray veil.

The cellar door was just opening as he reached it. His father stood there, a tall, lean figure with silver-gray hair and a well-groomed beard. Despite the situation, Richard Thompson was, as always, impeccably dressed in dark corduroy trousers and a checkered shirt that was meticulously tucked into the waistband. The orderliness of his appearance stood in sharp contrast to the chaos of the world around him.

He had always valued order and discipline, qualities that had accompanied him through a long career as a school principal—and that now, in the apocalypse, proved vital for survival. His strict attitude, which David had often perceived as stubborn and petty as a teenager, now appeared as an anchor in a world that had lost all structure.

"David. How are you?" asked Richard with a calm, controlled voice, but his eyes, the same green eyes that David saw in the mirror, betrayed his deep relief and joy.

"Thank you, I'm fine." David's voice broke slightly, overwhelmed by the emotion of the reunion. He stepped forward and hugged his father, felt the bony firmness of the older man, smelled the familiar scent of pipe tobacco and the aftershave he had used for decades. It was a smell from another time, a world of normality and routine that now seemed as distant as another planet.

"Where are the children and Eva? How are they?" asked his mother worriedly as she appeared behind his father from the cellar. Margaret Thompson was a small, delicate woman with a heart-shaped face that, despite her seventy years, showed surprisingly few wrinkles. Her normally carefully styled silver-gray hair, which she usually wore in a neat bun, now fell in untidy strands into her face, a sign of how much the events had thrown her off track too.

Her eyes, a warm chocolate brown, were however as lively and alert as ever. She wore a knitted vest over a blouse, whose once white color had now faded to an indefinable gray tone, and a plain dark trouser. Around her narrow shoulders was wrapped a handwoven blanket in the colors of the Thompson clan—dark green, blue, and red—an heirloom of her Scottish ancestors.

"They're with Ben. They're fine." David stepped forward and hugged his mother too, felt how her narrow shoulders trembled under his grip. She had become thinner, he noticed—they all had. The deprivation of the last weeks had taken its toll, had melted the flesh from their bones, had carved furrows into their faces that had not been there before the war.

"I'm so glad you're still alive. It's all so terrible," she said, no longer holding back the tears. They ran freely down her cheeks as she hugged her son even tighter, as if she could protect him from all harm by sheer force of will. "We were so worried! The news got worse and worse, and then everything collapsed, no more communication, no electricity, nothing…"

David stroked her back reassuringly, felt the small bones under his fingers, as fragile as the wings of a bird. "I know, Mum. We too. But now we're here, we're together. That's all that matters."

"And are you still staying in the cellar?" asked David, when they finally parted. He looked back at the open cellar door, from which a weak light shone—probably from candles or an oil lamp.

"Yes, we didn't know what the radiation was like," his father replied with a tired sigh. The burden of the past weeks was clearly visible in the deep furrows on his forehead, in the dark circles that lay like half-moons under his eyes. "The announcements on the radio spoke of deadly fallout, and we didn't want to take any risk."

"That was smart," David confirmed. "But the radiation here is now at a relatively safe level. Ben has a measuring device. The values are elevated, but not life-threatening. In the house about 2-3.8 millisieverts, outside up to about four."

His parents exchanged a look in which relief mingled with caution. They had spent the last two weeks almost exclusively in the cellar, only venturing upstairs for short, necessary trips—to the toilet, to get water, or to bring additional supplies down.

"Come down," said his father and made an inviting gesture toward the cellar door. "It's not much, but at least warm and safe."

They went down to the cellar together, a large, well-developed area that Richard had converted over the years into a kind of hobby workshop and storage room. Unlike at Ben's, where the cellar had retained its original, rustic character, this room had been carefully renovated. The walls were plastered and painted in a light beige, the floor covered with practical, gray-mottled tiles. Energy-saving LED lights hung from the ceiling, now dark without power, replaced by a circle of candles and two antique petroleum lamps, whose warm, flickering light bathed the room in a golden twilight.

Shelves of sturdy metal ran along all the walls, systematically filled with tools, household supplies, and—as David now noted with amazement—an impressive collection of emergency supplies.

White, large storage buckets from a well-known emergency food company stood everywhere in the cellar. They were neatly stacked, in a system that only his father could understand, labeled with waterproof markers indicating date and contents. There must have been dozens, maybe even over a hundred. Next to them were stacked boxes of water bottles, boxes of medications and first-aid equipment, tool sets, batteries, candles, matches, and countless other items that were of inestimable value in a world without functioning infrastructure.

"Man, you have a lot of supplies," said David, and his voice betrayed the mix of surprise and joy he felt. His father, often smiled at for his "survivalism," had been proven right, in the most tragic of all possible ways.

Richard shrugged, a gesture of feigned modesty that did not quite hide the satisfaction he felt. "I bought long-lasting emergency food over a year ago that should last two people for ten years," he said with a hint of pride in his voice. He had always believed in being prepared for the worst, had endured the little jibes from his sons and his wife, ignored the head-shaking of neighbors when he once again unloaded a delivery truck full of supplies. Now his caution had proven wise in a frightening way.

"For two people, ten years? So much? I can't believe it," said David and stared incredulously at the large white buckets that were stacked up to the ceiling. The sheer amount was overwhelming—a hoard of security in a destroyed world. David felt a deep gratitude toward his father, mixed with a hint of shame because he had so often smiled at those preparations.

"I always believed that the day would come when we would need this," Richard said quietly, while stroking one of the buckets with his hand, almost lovingly, like the head of a faithful dog. "Not necessarily a nuclear war. Maybe a virus, an economic collapse, a breakdown of supply systems. People think that our civilization is so robust, so immovable. But I taught history. I know how quickly everything can collapse, how thin the veneer of civilization actually is."

He was silent for a moment, his gaze directed into the distance, as if he were looking through the walls of the cellar into the past or perhaps the future. "Well, now we are eight, so it will last us two and a half years," he finally continued, shaking his head as if waking from a dream.

Margaret had set up a small camping table in the cellar, at which they now all took a seat. The tabletop was made of washable plastic, the surface slightly scratched from years of use on camping trips. The metallic table legs gave a soft, metallic clattering sound as they sat down.

"Most of it is freeze-dried stuff that lasts twenty-five years," Richard explained expertly, pointing to the stacked buckets. "Some tastes quite palatable, others are, well, an acquired taste. We've already tried quite a few."

He stood up and went to one of the buckets, opened the airtight lid, and took out a small package. It contained a brownish powder that remotely resembled instant coffee, only coarser and with visible pieces in it.

"This here, for example, is supposed to be beef with potatoes," he said with a crooked smile as he held up the packet. "Tastes more like salty cardboard with potato flavor, but it keeps you alive."

Margaret twisted her face into a grimace. "It's really horrible," she confirmed with a slight shudder. "But your father has also acquired some cans of actual meat and real beans. We ration those strictly for special occasions."

David couldn't believe how lucky they were that his father had been so foresighted and had bought so much emergency food. In a world where people were now fighting for every can and starving, this cellar was a true treasure. It was enough that it would last for their entire family—including Ben, Sandra, and the children—for two and a half. With sparing allocation, rationed to the bare necessities, perhaps even for more then two and half years.

Two and a half years in which they wouldn't have to desperately search for food. Two and a half years in which they could concentrate on other things—like building a new existence, learning the skills they would need in this new, harsh world. It was an invaluable advantage in a game whose rules had been rewritten overnight.

He sat down with his parents at the camping table, whose orange plastic surface bore the marks of countless family outings and garden parties. In another time, he would have found this table old-fashioned and ugly. Now it seemed to him like the most beautiful sight in the world—a piece of stability in a crumbling reality.

"The radiation outside is so low that one can stay there," said David, as he took off his jacket and hung it over the back of the folding chair. "Ben has a radiation measuring device. In the house it's about 2-3.8 millisieverts, outside about 4. Higher than normal, but not deadly."

His parents exchanged a glance in which relief mingled with caution.

"We weren't sure," said Margaret, nervously plucking at the sleeve of her dark blue wool sweater. "The radio broadcasts stopped about a week ago, and since then we've been sitting here in the dark—figuratively speaking."

"With us too," David confirmed. "I think the provisional transmitters have failed. Or maybe there's no one left to broadcast." He didn't want to say aloud what they were all thinking: that the last remnants of organized government or military that had maintained the emergency broadcasts might also have been destroyed.

An uncomfortable silence spread as each of them considered the implications of this possibility. If there was no organized government anymore, no central authority, what would become of them? Would humanity fall back into a state of war of all against all, as Thomas Hobbes had once described it—"solitary, poor, nasty, brutish, and short"?

"There must still be someone somewhere," Richard finally said, breaking the silence. "The government has bunkers, emergency plans. They will come back. It will take time, but they will come back."

David nodded, though he wasn't sure if he actually believed it. He respected his father's belief in the institutions, the order. It was a belief that had carried him throughout his career as a teacher and later principal—the belief that the state, despite its flaws and weaknesses, ultimately acted for the benefit of its citizens. But this belief was hard to justify in the firestorms of nuclear war.

David let his gaze wander through the cellar. The systematic order, the stock of food, the careful planning—all typical of his father, who had been a planner all his life, a man of routines and precautions. Many of the neighborhood children had mocked Mr. Thompson with his endless safety rules and his "bunker." But who was mocking now?

"We should consider all moving in together," David

said after a while. "Together we are stronger. And it would be better for the children to have their grandparents around them."

His parents nodded in agreement. The thought of having their grandchildren with them seemed to visibly please them. It would not only bring practical advantages but also emotional stability in a world that had lost all stability.

"But where?" asked Margaret. "Here or at Ben's?"

David thought for a moment. Both places had their advantages and disadvantages. Ben's house was closer to the sea, which would allow fishing when the preserved supplies ran out. But his parents' house had more space, a better-developed cellar, and above all the extensive supplies. So he decided to talk to the others. The best would probably be at his parents'.

EPILOGUE: A WORLD OF ASHES

After about a week and a half, the war was over. Neither side was able to fight anymore; the nuclear exchange had brought both superpowers to their knees. The command structures were shattered, the communication lines interrupted, the infrastructure destroyed. What remained were isolated islands of military power—a general here, a fleet commander there, each now his own ruler over a shrinking realm of ruins and despair.

The world had transformed into a patchwork of chaos and anarchy. The fine lines on maps that once separated nations from each other had now become meaningless. Power redefined itself, was measured in water supplies, ammunition, medicine, and the ability to apply or defend against violence.

Millions of American citizens fled to Mexico, streamed across the border that had once been so heavily guarded to prevent immigration. Now it was reversed—the former inhabitants of the most powerful nation in the world became desperate refugees, willing to sacrifice everything for the chance of survival. From Mexico, many tried to make their way further to South America, driven by rumors of untouched cities, intact civilizations, food, and security.

Not all reached this promised land. The roads were dangerous, dominated by gangs and self-proclaimed warlords who considered every traveler as a potential resource—as labor, as goods, as organ donor, or simply as food. The stories that emerged from this region became increasingly horrific, until they finally fell silent as the last communication paths collapsed.

In Europe, a similarly grim picture emerged. Switzerland, long praised as a bastion of neutrality and stability, now showed a different face. The Swiss Army, once a symbol of precision and discipline, fired mercilessly into the masses of people who desperately tried to reach the supposed security of the Alpine fortress.

Apocalyptic scenes played out at the borders to Switzerland. Hundreds of thousands of Italian, German, and French refugees, many of them heavily irradiated, with pain-contorted faces and peeling skin, were met with machine gun fire. The tender threads of humanity that had connected peoples and nations for decades tore under the pressure of pure survival will.

"Switzerland is too small for all these people," was the official justification that was sent over the last remaining military frequencies. "We don't have enough resources for our own population, let alone for millions of strangers. Most are doomed to die anyway—from radiation, from hunger, from cold. We grant them a quick, merciful death."

However, there was no mercy to be felt as the heavy machine guns fired their deadly staccato into the crowd, as women, children, old people collapsed under the hail of bullets, their bodies piled up like sandbags into grotesque barricades, behind which the next wave of desperate refugees hid.

The few medications that still existed were inadequate for the masses of wounded and radiation sick. The large pharmaceutical factories, once proud of their ability to produce healing and relief for the ailments of humanity, had now themselves become radioactive ruins. What medicines still existed were either hidden in the cellars of hospitals, hoarded in the bunker facilities of the powerful, or in the hands of unscrupulous black market dealers who raised their prices with the desperation of their customers.

In Germany, once the economic powerhouse of Europe, parts of the Bundeswehr had broken away from their chain of command. Soldiers who had belonged to the former Bundeswehr moved in small, well-armed troops through the devastated landscape. They had forgotten or denied their original mission—the protection of the population. Instead, they became the robber barons of the atomic age.

They shot residents of villages whose houses were still intact and quartered themselves in their dwellings. Families were driven out or killed, their supplies confiscated, their women and daughters degraded to sex slaves. The uniform, once a symbol of duty and honor, became the mark of oppression, before which the survivors trembled.

Similar scenes played out in the other parts of former NATO Europe. The military structure, once a finely tuned system of chains of command and responsibilities, had degenerated into a loose network of armed gangs, each led by an officer or non-commissioned officer who had declared himself ruler over his small territory.

In the USA, no real army existed anymore. The proud armed forces that had once held the world in suspense were shattered, atomized, reduced to their basic components. But parts of the leadership staff of the US armed forces and crews of the missile silos, ships, and nuclear submarines still functioned, connected by fragmented communication lines and the iron will for revenge.

Again and again, they could still carry out nuclear attacks against Russia—from hidden silos in the Midwest, from submerged submarines in the depths of the oceans, from secret bases that had survived even in the nuclear inferno. They were desperate, senseless blows against an enemy who was already just as much on the ground as they themselves. But revenge and retaliation were powerful drivers, especially in a world that had lost every other meaning.

The global situation deteriorated rapidly. Wars and conflicts broke out everywhere on earth —no longer the well-organized conflicts with state-of-the-art technology from pre-war times, but primitive, brutal fights over the most basic resources: water, food, fuel, protection from the elements. The nuclear winter, which globally lowered temperatures by 11 to 22 degrees, exacerbated the situation. Harvests failed, livestock starved or froze, water sources froze over.

More famines followed, worse than anything humanity had ever experienced before. People ate tree bark, grass, rats, finally each other. The world population fell rapidly and reached its lowest point after seven years at 245 million—a fraction of the 8.5 billion who had populated the Earth before the war.

Only then, slowly and hesitantly, did the survivors begin to hope again. The radiation decreased, the nuclear winter gave way to a radioactive spring. First plants began to grow again, mutated to be sure and often poisonous, but at least a sign that nature was recovering. People learned which plants were edible and which deadly, which animals could be hunted and how to protect themselves from the mutated predators that now populated the ruins of the cities.

New communities formed, small and isolated at first, connected by kinship, common origin, or simply the coincidences of survival. From these seeds of community developed, over time, new forms of social organization—some democratic and cooperative, others feudalistic or tyrannical. Humanity began its long, arduous journey back to civilization.

The population number rose again, slowly at first, then faster, as survival conditions improved. A new generation was born, children who had never known the old world, for whom atomic craters and radiation zones were as natural as mountains and rivers had been for their ancestors.

These children grew up with the stories of their parents and grandparents—stories of a world where light appeared at the touch of a button, where machines flew through the air, where food was available in seemingly endless abundance. They heard these stories with the same mixture of awe and disbelief with which earlier generations had listened to the myths of Atlantis or El Dorado.

The reality they knew was harder, more primitive, but also in some ways purer. They knew the value of a drop of clean water, a piece of unirradiated land, a handful of viable seeds. They understood what their ancestors had forgotten: that the Earth was not inexhaustible, that technology could be a double-edged sword, that power without wisdom led to downfall.

Whether they would learn from these lessons, whether the new civilization that slowly emerged from the ashes of the old would be wiser, more cautious, more humane—that was written in the stars, in the same stars that had indifferently looked down upon the self-destruction of the former masters of the Earth.

The history of humanity continued, changed, marked, but not ended. The lesson of the Great Fire, as the nuclear war was soon called, had been dearly bought. Whether it had been understood, only time would tell.

Printed in Dunstable, United Kingdom